The Adventures of Lily

Darcy J. Busch

PublishAmerica
Baltimore

First printing

All characters in this book are fictitious, and any resemblance to real persons, living or dead, is coincidental.

ISBN: 1-4241-8473-8
PUBLISHED BY PUBLISHAMERICA, LLLP
www.publishamerica.com
Baltimore

Printed in the United States of America

To my husband Tim and my daughter Cami for all of their patience while I was busy writing this book and also going to college. Also to the Chora girls; my nieces in Salina, Kansas, for all of their help reading my manuscript to make sure it would be successful. To my nephew Jeffrey, also in Salina. I want also to dedicate this book to the memory of my little guy, Connor Pearce. Not a day goes by that I don't miss seeing your beautiful little face.

To anyone who has a dream—with a little hard work, a dream can become a reality!

Chapter One
The Tree

This is a story that began a very long time ago, even longer than your great, great, great grandparents births. This mystic place was known as the Great Unknown Tree. At one time, this place was full of mischievous little creatures called Taemites. The Taemites looked like little men with horns in the place where ears are normally located. These unusual creatures were covered with fur and feather like hair. Each creature's color was different, because this was a way of displaying which Taemites were more powerful than others. The strange thing about Taemites is that they were quite full of magical powers and were extremely dangerous to the survival of human beings. The story of the Taemites might have been lost forever if not for the act of one brave little girl named Lily Wright.

The day began as a normal day for twelve-year-old Lily Wright, except the fate of this young girl was already set in motion. Today would be the day that would change her life forever. Lily lived in Scott City; a small little town in western Kansas. This twelve-year-old girl was not a typical child, because she had been given a special gift that very few individuals were aware that she actually possessed. Lily always had dreams. Not just a typical, run of the mill, normal dream. These dreams often held hidden messages, which were extremely valuable in each of Lily's cases in which she spent numerous hours investigating. She was constantly imagining what her next escapade would be. Lily was getting ready for an adventure outdoors, because it was summer break and school was dismissed. Lily had been dreaming about what detective work she could find to investigate. As she often did, Lily ate her breakfast quickly and was out the door. The day was about to begin that would bring Lily face to face with the Taemites and all of the mystery that surrounds them.

Lily walked to her best friend Nick's house to ask if he wanted to be a part of her adventure. Lily and Nick have been friends ever since they met at kindergarten. Since then, the two had been inseparable. Nick was the more practical of this duo. More times than not, it was Nick that objected to some of Lily's outrageous ideas. Nick only lived a couple blocks from Lily's house, which made it very easy to just pop over whenever the need arose.

"Hi. I think today's the day that we find our big mystery!" Lily exclaimed.

"What do you think we'll find?" Nick asked.

"I'm not sure, but it's going to be really exciting and, besides, I'll know when I see it. I think the best place to find mysteries is to go over to the south side of town," Lily said, hoping this would not scare Nick, because the south side of town was known to have strange, unexplained events occurring daily. Scott City was a small little town, but even so there were many unexplained occurrences that happened frequently.

"I don't think that's a good idea," Nick said, trying not to let Lily know he was a little frightened.

"You can go home if you want, but I'm going," Lily replied.

"No, I'm not afraid and, besides, you can't go all by yourself, it's too dangerous for girls."

"I am the bravest person in the whole world and nothing scares me!" Lily scolded Nick. Nick often made those statements just to remind Lily that she was a girl.

"Fine, then let's go!"

They decided to ride their bikes since it was quite a ways to the land full of mysteries.

The ride did not last more than half an hour when they finally arrived at the junkyard, which was just one of the many places full of unexplained phenomena. This junkyard had been abandoned for several years. The previous owners had heard strange sounds coming from the forest behind it.

Once Lily and Nick got the fence jarred loose so they could enter, the adventure was now only moments from beginning.

"Let's go look in that little building over by the woods," Lily said. The door was locked, but that never stopped this brave detective. "Nick, help me put this crate against the wall so I can crawl in through the window," Lily ordered.

"There, now put your foot on my hand, Lily, and I can help you," Nick said, still not so sure that this was such a good idea.

"Okay, I'm in. Go to the door and I will let you in," she told Nick. Lily's heart began to beat faster in anticipation of what they might soon discover.

Inside, it was pretty dark, but detective Lily always came prepared. She opened up her backpack and set out three of her handy, never failed her flashlights. "Now that we can see, let's find out about all of the hidden secrets in this building," Lily said.

Nick looked in a dusty old file cabinet, but only newspapers were inside. "Nothing in here except really old papers," Nick said disappointingly.

Lily found a small wooden box with a picture of a tree on it. "Hey, look at this!" Lily exclaimed.

"That's nothing but a stupid box!" yelled Nick.

"No, it's not! Listen, there's something inside." Lily took out another one of her important investigative tools she always kept in her backpack. She pried the box open, and inside was a red book and a small mirror.

"Why do suppose that was in the box for?" Nick asked.

"I don't know, but I'm definitely going to find out!" Lily replied. Nick picked up the book and opened it and out fell a necklace. "Look, Lily, this necklace has a pendant shaped like a tree, just like what's on the top of that old box," Nick said eagerly awaiting a reply from his partner in this adventure.

"Hey, Nick, you said there was only newspapers in that file cabinet, right?' Lily asked.

"Yeah, but that's not gonna help us, will it?" Nick said, not sure what Lily was thinking. Lily went to the file cabinet and opened it.

"Let's see what information we can deduct from the these old papers!" Lily exclaimed. She began flipping through several of the papers, but nothing seemed to stand out. Just as Lily was about to shut the file cabinet, she noticed one newspaper that had been written on. "Hey, look at this. I bet there is some information in this newspaper that can explain what is happening here," Lily said.

Nick quickly walked over to where Lily was standing.

Lily noticed the date on the paper was May 12, 1877. "Wow, I didn't even know they had newspapers way back then," Lily said.

"Of course they did. Don't you remember in Mr. Fox's history class that we learned about the creation of newspapers and how important they are in recording valuable information?" Nick replied.

"Oh, yeah, I was just seeing if you remembered," Lily said, trying to cover her embarrassment. "Look, right here in this article it says that on May 2, 1877, a man named John Howard was found badly beaten and bloody. It says that the man claimed he was attacked by some strange looking creatures and they killed his wife and daughter and abducted his son, but somehow he managed to free himself; unable to save his family from such horrific deaths," Lily reported. As she continued reading, the column stated that the sheriff did not believe him and he was tried for the murder of his family.

"Do you think he really killed his family?' Nick asked.

"I don't know, but I do know where we can find out more about this interesting case," Lily told Nick.

"Where?" Nick asked.

"At the library. Remember Mrs. Blackburn told us at our school library that all records of past events are kept documented at all local libraries," informed Lily.

They quickly got back on their bikes and were headed toward the library to fill in some questions about this unusual case.

Nick and Lily arrived at the library and went running inside. "Okay, now where do we start?" Nick asked.

"Well, I guess we need to ask the librarian for some help," Lily replied.

They walked up to the front desk and asked Ms. Carroll where to find research of a past event that had occurred in Scott City.

"Why on earth do you want know that for? Don't you both want to be playing outside instead of being cooped up in here?" Ms. Carroll asked.

"No, this is sorta research for a summer assignment for school," reported detective Lily.

"Well, okay, down stairs in the basement is where all of the old documents are stored," Ms. Carroll said.

"Thanks," Nick and Lily said in unison.

Once they were downstairs the detective work resumed. The room was full of boxes of newspapers. Unlike some of the larger libraries, Scott City's library was rather small and had not filed these documents onto a computer system yet.

"We're never going to be able to go through all of these boxes!" Nick complained.

"All we have to do is look for papers dated for May 1877 and later," Lily calmly said.

After what seemed like hours, Lily found the box for which they were looking. "Hey, Nick, here it is! This newspaper says that during the trial of John Howard many strange events occurred frequently in the jail where he was being held. At first it was just things being thrown against the walls right outside his jail cell. The weird thing was that nobody actually saw who or what was throwing these items. Later, as the trial progressed, lawyer after lawyer were physically attacked by dark figures in the night. The last event that happened was the death of the judge. Nobody knows exactly how it happened, but the judge had a picture of a tree that he had grasped in his hand. The sheriff decided to hang Howard; regardless of the fact that he was locked up behind bars and could not possibly have been involved. The fact that all of those strange occurrences began after Howard was arrested only made the act of hanging more appropriate," Lily finished reading.

"Do you think the box we found belonged to John Howard?" Nick asked.

"That's exactly who it belonged to! I think the picture of a tree the judge had in his hand has something to do with that box we found. Let's get back to the junkyard and find out more about this mystery of John Howard," Lily ordered her partner. It was time to return to the land of mysteries.

When Nick and Lily got back to their bikes, they noticed it was beginning to get dark.

"Lily, I'm sorry, but I have to get home so my mom won't worry. Can we continue this investigation tomorrow?" Nick asked, hoping she would not go on without him.

"Yeah, you're right, it's getting late. I'll meet you at your house tomorrow morning at 8:00, and you better be ready if you want to keep being my partner!" Lily replied.

"Okay, see you in the morning."

Lily went home and ate supper with her family and went straight to bed. It had been a very busy day and she was extremely tired. Lily fell right to sleep, and soon began dreaming about the mystery of the tree.

The dream was about the trial of John Howard and she was sitting in the very same courtroom. As Lily watched the attorney ask John Howard many questions, she noticed that in the back of the room was a short, odd looking individual covered in a brown cloak. Just as Lily was about to go up to talk with this strange looking character; he got up quickly and ran out of the door. Lily followed him, but when she reached the hall he was nowhere to be seen. Lily turned around to return to the courtroom and noticed something lying on the floor. It was a weird shaped key.

Suddenly, Lily woke up from her dream. Sitting up in her bed, she knew this was an important clue to solving the mystery behind John Howard.

Lily arrived at Nick's house at exactly 8:00 in the morning and, much to her surprise, he was waiting for her.

"Hi Nick. How did you sleep?" Lily asked.

"I didn't sleep good at all. My mind kept thinking about John Howard. How about you?" Nick asked.

"I had a dream about his trial. I was in the courtroom where John Howard was being tried for the murder of his family and I noticed a strange looking creature covered in a brown cloak in the back of the courtroom, so I followed him and he just disappeared. However, I did find an odd shaped key where he had been standing," Lily replied excitedly.

"It was only a dream. It doesn't mean anything," Nick replied.

"Oh, I absolutely know it meant that we have another clue to search for at the junkyard."

Although Nick knew better than to question the bizarre thinking of Lily; he decided something needed to be said about this once and for all. "I know you believe in the hidden meanings of dreams, but I think that even for you this is a little too weird. It was only a dream, nothing else." Nick tried to convince Lily of his belief.

"Nick, everything about this investigation is weird. Why is so hard to believe that I received a message from someone from the past?" Lily pleaded for Nick to have faith in her. "We need to find that key in order to get closer to solving this case," Lily continued.

"I hope you know what you're doing, this is beginning to sound dangerous to me," Nick said.

The two detectives rode off for the junkyard and toward the mystery awaiting them.

Lily and Nick arrived at the junkyard, but to their surprise they found an old, beatup truck parked at the gate.

"Who do you think that is?" Nick asked.

"I don't know, but let's get a closer look at him," Lily replied.

14

They quietly got closer to the stranger.

"Oh you're not going to believe this! It looks like how John Howard looked in my dream," Lily said.

"What? Lily, remember I told you it was only a dream and it wasn't real," Nick tried to convince his partner.

"I don't care what you think Nick, but that's John Howard."

"You're crazy Lily; John Howard would be dead. He was alive way back in 1877."

Lily always tuned Nick out when he didn't agree with her. "Look, he's putting a box into the building," Lily reported.

The duo continued spying on this mysterious person. Finally, the stranger left, so Lily and Nick once again went into the little building.

Once inside, the detective work resumed. Lily found the newly placed box and pried it open with one of her tools. The box was full of small bones.

"What kind of bones are those, Lily?"

"I don't know, but we've got to continue our search for solving this mystery," Lily said.

The investigation continued, but not much evidence was found. Lily and Nick went back to the file cabinet to have another look at it.

"Hey, Nick, help me move this. It looks like there's something under this file cabinet," Lily said excitingly.

The excitement was building when Lily found an old, dusty map directly under the cabinet. As Lily carefully unfolded this newly discovered item, she noticed that it was an old map of Kansas. The map had certain areas marked for some unexplained reason.

"Nick, go get the book we found yesterday," Lily ordered.

"Okay, here it is. Why do you want it?"

Lily opened the book up, and in the middle she found where a page had been torn out. "Now, let's see if this map came from this book." Lily discovered that in fact the map had come from that same book.

Nick and Lily knew this was another important clue. They continued searching in order to find more answers to this puzzling case.

Nick found another box in the corner that he hadn't seen before. Inside, much to his surprise, he found a key shaped like a tree. "Hey, Lily, look at this!"

Lily ran over to Nick's side. "See, it's the same key I saw in my dream!"

"What do you think the key is for?" Nick asked.

"I don't know, let's keep looking. There's got to be something we're overlooking."

As Nick continued with the search, Lily went over to a table and laid out everything they had found. Looking carefully at each piece of evidence, she figured out what had been in front of them this whole time. Lily picked up the book and tried to read what was written inside. The words were written in some kind of strange code. Suddenly, Lily picked up the mirror and held it up by the writing in the book. "Hey, Nick, come here, you've got to see this!" Lily exclaimed. "Look, if you read the reflection of the words in the mirror it makes sense."

The clues were beginning to come together. As Lily held the mirror, Nick read the words.

"The tree in the woods is where the Taemites live. These creatures are extremely dangerous to people. The only possible protection from the Taemites is by using the crystal pendant. The pendant is made from lazenfront. Lazenfront is a highly toxic chemical for Taemites. Fortunately, lazenfront is not toxic to humans. Now what do we do?" Nick asked Lily, even though he knew what her answer was going to be.

"Nick, do I really need to say it? We're going into the woods."

The detectives gathered up all of their needed supplies and walked into the forest.

The woods seemed darker and the two friends heard strange noises coming from everywhere. "I'm scared, Lily, are you?"

"No, I'm not, but we're going to have to be brave in order to solve this mystery," Lily said, trying to convince Nick, even though she was a little scared herself. Lily took out a couple of flashlights from her backpack; making it easier for them to see better. "The map shows the tree where the Taemites live is by a large stone shaped like a mushroom," Lily reported to Nick.

The trip in the woods seemed to last hours and they still had not found the stone. Nick and Lily grew exhausted from all of the walking and were just about to turn around and go home, when, right before their eyes…was the stone. Just like the map showed, there was a huge tree covered with moss and vines.

"Nick, help me look for the door. It's got to be here somewhere."

The two searched the tree for the door.

Suddenly Lily touched part of the tree and the door suddenly appeared. "It's locked! Wait! Remember, we found that key," she exclaimed. Lily reached into her backpack and removed the key. It fit perfectly, and before long the duo was inside this strange looking fortress.

Once they were inside, Lily decided she had better put on the necklace in order to keep them safe from the Taemites. Inside, the tree was like a maze. Lily and Nick kept going in circles.

"Wait, Nick, this isn't working! Let's get out the mirror and see if it can help us again." Lily retrieved the mirror and held it up in front of a wall. Suddenly she noticed the reflection changed from what they were actually seeing. Instead of just seeing a wall, they saw a door with another picture of a tree. "Nick, you better stay behind me since I am wearing this necklace!" Lily ordered.

"I don't think this is a good idea," Nick replied.

"We have to uncover this mystery for the safety of our families, and for the people who live in Scott City," Lily reminded Nick.

As Lily and Nick went inside, the door suddenly closed directly behind them.

"Nick, did you close that?" Lily asked.

"No, I didn't."

They both were a little scared now, but knew they couldn't turn back now.

Inside was a long hall with a door at the end. Once Lily and Nick walked through the door, they entered another hall. The walls were covered with what appeared to be small mirrors with the letter "T" engraved on them. Alongside each wall was a door, but inside each room was a mystery just waiting for the two detectives to come and solve them.

"I don't understand. This is only a tree, why does it seem so big in here?" Nick asked.

"It's the magic of the Taemites. Okay, it's time to see the Taemites up close and personal," Lily said bravely.

The two continued with this exploration.

The room was fairly large, and in the corner was another large box. Lily took out another one of her tools and pried the lid open. Inside were stairs leading into blackness and into the land of the unknown.

Nick and Lily went down the stairs to find the answers to their questions.

"What are we going to do if we find the Taemites?" Nick asked.

"I don't know," Lily responded.

At the bottom of the stairs was a large book that had been opened up to a specific page.

Nick read the writing in the book:

The Taemites are not as powerful as they once were. A long time ago, the Taemites were made strong due to curious humans. People would enter the Taemites territory and, once inside, the Taemites would look them directly in the eyes and this would vaporize the humans. Each person that was vaporized would give more strength to the Taemites. Finally, one day a young boy was brought to the tree. The Taemites raised the young child. This boy was called the Chosen One, because he had the mark of a Taemite on his face. The mark was a birthmark shaped like a tree. As the Chosen One grew, he learned all of the magical powers the Taemites practiced. Once the Chosen One was a man; he began to question how he had come to live in the tree. The Chosen One went to the Taemite that was, essentially, his mother. She telepathically told him what had happened to his family. Upon discovering the answer to his question, he grew angry with the Taemites and one by one began using the very same magic that the Taemites had taught him to put an end to these dangerous creatures, or so he believed. When the Taemites all were destroyed, he placed them in a box and buried them in a deep hole in the woods.

The two investigators were immersed in what they were reading in the book and were not aware of how late it had become. Their families were growing more concerned for the safety of Lily and Nick. Eventually the police were called to drive around town to try and find this missing duo.

The police drove all over Scott City and eventually tracked down their bicycles at the junkyard. Nobody knew exactly where Lily and Nick were, so the local TV reporters from Garden City were sent out to make a plea to the public for any information leading to the safe return of the children.

By now a large crowd of observers was growing around this abandoned location. Both of the families were extremely upset and wanted to get all the help available. In fact, Lily's grandfather came out to help with the search.

Her grandfather used to be a detective and was ready to jump into action in search of his granddaughter. Lily wanted to become a detective just like her grandpa. He often shared his advice on how to become an excellent detective. Both Lily and Nick's mothers were feeling overwhelmed with fear for the safety of their children.

While all of this activity was carrying on at the edge of the woods, a dark figure wearing a brown cloak was watching. The figure turned around and returned to his place in the woods; the very same place in which Lily and Nick were inside investigating.

The police, along with Grandpa, decided to move the search into the woods after looking everywhere in the junkyard.

Unaware of the large crowd just outside of the woods, Nick and Lily finished reading most of the book and were ready to continue on with their search for John Howard.

"Well, Nick, looks like we don't have to worry about finding the Taemites," Lily replied happily.

"So, do you think that those bones in the box were really the Taemites?" Nick asked.

"Definitely, but now we need to find out what happened to the son of John Howard," Lily said, really wondering if they ever would learn about him.

The two walked on past the book and found yet another room. Inside, the young sleuths found a bed and a desk with a kerosene lamp.

"It looks like someone lives in here. Do you think they still are here somewhere?" Nick asked growing a bit uneasy with what the answer might be.

Lily walked over to the desk and found a small book. She opened it up and discovered it belonged to the Chosen One. Inside Lily read:

> *My family was murdered by the Taemites, and my father was killed by humans. My life is not normal. I feel betrayed by the Taemites, even by my mother Taemite. What am I?*

"Do you think that is John Howard's son?" Nick asked, even though he already knew the answer.

"Yes, I think it must be," Lily said.

After reading the book, Lily reached to touch the lamp. It was still warm. "I think the Chosen One lives in this tree, and he is somewhere pretty close. Let's keep moving," Lily ordered.

Just as the two were leaving the room, Lily and Nick turned around and right before their eyes they saw a dark looking figure standing in the hallway. Lily and Nick were very terrified, but suddenly Lily remembered her dream. This was the same figure she had seen before and now she felt he would not hurt them.

Lily slowly walked over to the Chosen One and asked if he was the son of John Howard. The figure nodded his head. "It's okay, we won't hurt you. We are here to help," Lily said softly.

Nick walked over to the figure and pulled down the hood and they both saw a man with a lot of facial hair and long curly black hair. This man appeared to be part human and part animal. Even though this man did not look normal, Lily and Nick sat down to find out how they could help him.

"What's your name?" Lily asked.

"The Taemites called me the Chosen One," the creature said.

"No, I mean the name your real family use to call you. Do you remember?" Lily asked, very caring.

"My name is..." he struggled, but he just couldn't remember.

"It's okay, we'll help you remember," Lily said.

The young detectives began searching his room again, trying to find anything that belonged to him before his family was killed.

Nick yelled in excitement, "Look, it's a teddy bear and on the tag it says he belongs to Michael Howard."

The new friends were jumping up and down with joy from the excitement of finding the truth about this hidden secret.

"Now we know your name, but how is it you aren't old?" Lily asked.

"The Taemites used their magic to make me stay this age," Michael responded.

"So you can do magic?" Lily asked.

"Yes, but I will only use it for doing good deeds," Michael added.

"Why did all sorts of weird things happen at your Dad's trial?" Nick asked.

"That was the Taemites trying to get them to kill John Howard. The Taemites wanted him dead so I would not have any family left," Michael responded sadly.

Amazingly enough, the reason no one could see the Taemites as they tortured John Howard was simple. The Taemites used their magical powers to become invisible to humans. The mystery was now officially solved.

"Well, the best is yet to come, because now you can come out of this tree and live a normal life with people," Nick said excitedly.

"No, I can't. This is my home. My family is gone and I don't want to leave this place," Michael said.

As the friends spent time together, they heard voices coming from outside. They quickly went to the door and noticed there were police outside.

"Hey, Lily, isn't that your grandpa with the police?" Nick asked.

"Oh no! We are going to be in a lot of trouble with our families. Well, Michael, we are going to keep your secret so nobody will bother you," Lily said.

Before Nick and Lily left, the duo ran and gave Michael a hug and told him they would return for visits. The two young detectives very carefully exited the tree and found the police and Grandpa.

Grandpa brought Lily and Nick out from the woods to their loving families. Even though both families were ecstatic of the safe return of Lily and Nick, the adults had been extremely worried.

The worst part of being in trouble with parents is the waiting to see what the punishment is actually going to be.

The police never did learn about the tree, or even the secret of Michael Howard.

As for Lily and Nick…they had more cases to solve, but for now they needed to be with their families.

Chapter Two
The Mystery of the New Neighbor

Lily had spent the last several weeks grounded in her bedroom because she had stayed outside too late and scared her family. This didn't bother Lily, since she had actually solved her very first case. The problem with Lily was, that even after getting into a lot of trouble from her last adventure, she was already dreaming about her next.

One day, Lily was lying on her bed dreaming about her next quest when she heard a tap on her window. This startled her back into reality. Lily opened the curtain and, much to her surprise, it was her partner Nick.

"Hey, Lily, when can you come back outside?" Nick asked.

"This is my last day of being grounded. What have you been doing?" Lily eagerly asked.

Nick told her that he had been back up to visit Michael Howard.

This really made Lily angry. "You know you have to be careful that no one sees you. We have to keep him a secret!" Lily scolded.

"I know, I know. What's going to be our next case to investigate?" Nick asked, trying to change the subject.

"Tomorrow we'll ride around town on our bikes and see what we can find," Lily responded.

"Sounds good to me. See you later," Nick said as he rode off to look around by himself.

Lily went back to her daydreaming.

While Nick was riding around, he noticed a family moving in a few houses down from Lily's home. Instead of going on in search of a new mystery, he decided to stay and watch this new family. The new neighbors had a lot of boxes; so Nick decided he would be nice and asked if they needed some help.

"Hi, my name's Nick Masters. I live a few blocks down from here."

"Hi, Nick, my name is Jim Young and this is my wife Linda, and my daughter Brianna. I think we could use the help if you really don't mind," Mr. Young answered.

"Just tell me what you want me to do," Nick said.

The results of this act of kindness left Nick tired from moving boxes and furniture all afternoon. When everything was moved inside, Mrs. Young asked Nick to stay and have some lemonade.

The detective mode set in once Nick was inside the house, but nothing seemed unusual. This was the house that nobody had ever lived in for very long. The word around Scott City was that this house was haunted from a death that had occurred back in the 1950s. Nick decided this should be the next mystery to solve with his partner Lily. He said goodbye to the Youngs, got back on his bike and continued on with his ride.

As the day continued on, Nick kept thinking about the mystery of the Young's house.

Nick went home to eat dinner with his family and went to bed early so he could fill Lily in on what their next case to solve would be.

Bright and early the next morning Nick went over to Lily's house.

"Hi, Lily. Are you ready to begin our next investigation?" Nick asked.

"What's our next mystery?" Lily replied.

"Well, yesterday after I left your house, I noticed that you have new neighbors moving in a few houses down from here."

Before he could continue, Lily interrupted, and said, "I know, they are the Young family. They moved here from Texas. Their daughter Brianna is going to go to our school in the fall."

Nick broke in so he could resume his story. "Anyway, I think our next case should be to discover why no families live in that house for very long."

Lily thought about it for a while, then said, "Okay, let's get started."

The duo got on their bikes and rode down to the Young's house.

When they arrived, it appeared that nobody was there.

Lily decided to knock on the door anyway. As she was standing at the door, she peeked in through the window and noticed a strange looking picture leaning up against the wall in the living room. The picture appeared to be of a young couple with their dog. The way these people were dressed, it appeared to have been taken some time possibly in the 1950s. The strange thing about this photo was that the couple was standing in front of a house. The house looked exactly like this very same house.

Just as Lily was about to tell Nick of her discovery, Brianna came to the door.

"Hi, my name is Lily and this is my friend Nick," Lily said.

"I know Nick, I met him yesterday," Brianna replied.

"I thought maybe you might like to have some visitors since you're new in town," Lily said.

"Sure. Do you want to come inside?" Brianna asked.

The new friends went into Brianna's room to talk.

"Well, Brianna, why did you move from Texas?" Nick asked.

"We had to leave because of my dad's work," Brianna answered.

"What does your dad do?" Lily asked.

"He does detective work for the police."

This intrigued the sleuths very much. "How exciting!"

The new friends continued their conversation, and after a while decided to go into the kitchen for something to drink.

They passed the picture Lily had seen earlier, and Lily asked Brianna, "Who are those people in that picture?"

"I don't know, it was left behind by whoever lived here last." Eager to change the subject, Brianna asked if her friends would like some Pepsi.

When Lily and Nick finished their drinks, they said they needed to get home. Before leaving, Lily asked if they could come back tomorrow. Brianna was happy to have made new friends and agreed to see them the next day.

Lily and Nick got back on their bikes to ride over to Nick's home.

Once inside Nick's house, Lily eagerly admitted how curious she was about the picture in the living room. "Hey, Nick, who do you think the people were in the picture?" Lily asked.

"Probably the last owners. Lily, do you think that house is really haunted?" Nick said.

"If it is, we need to spend the night with Brianna to find out the truth," Lily said, trying to sound brave.

Lily and Nick both had heard the stories about that house, especially around Halloween. The stories always involved the death of a woman and her son. Back in the 1950s, a family moved into that house. This family appeared to be a normal family, except for the fact that the mother and son were rarely seen outdoors. Most of the neighbors believed they were just private people and did not disturb them. One night, in fact, it was the night before Halloween; the neighbors heard loud voices. It sounded like the family was having an argument. Later that night, the father threw a suitcase into the trunk of his car and took off. The next day, some of the neighbors went over to check on the mother and son, but no one answered the frantic knocks on the door. Eventually the police were called out and entered the house. The house was completely empty except for traces of what appeared to be blood in the kitchen. An investigation began on the disappearance of the mother and son. Years went by and the two were never found. When the father was found, he was arrested for the death of his family. He was found guilty during his trial and was sentenced to life in prison.

"Well, I think we need to find out about the first family who lived in that house. In fact, I bet my grandma might know something about them and the mystery surrounding that house."

The duo got back on their bikes and rode over to Lily's grandmother's house.

Lily and Nick greeted Grandma and knew she would offer them some milk and cookies. The best part about visiting her grandma was the cookies.

Once they finished their cookies, they began asking Grandma questions about the neighbor's house.

"Grandma, did you know the first family that moved into the haunted house down the street from my house?' Lily asked.

"My goodness, why do you young folks say such things?"

Lily continued her investigation. "That's the story on the street. Anyway, did you know the first family, the mother and son that were killed by the father?"

Grandma paused for a moment, then continued. "I saw them, but they were very private people. I was one of the neighbors concerned for them and went over to check on the mother and son the next morning. The police told me that nobody was in the house. They said the kitchen was covered in blood. The next five years our neighborhood was frightened because we believed the father had killed the mother and son. We thought he might come back to get revenge on some of us for getting the police involved."

The two young detectives sat in disbelief as Grandma finished her story.

"I guess the stories are true then?" Nick said.

"Yes, but why are you both wanting to hear about this horrible story?" Grandma asked.

"We think it is about time to solve this mystery. Besides, we met the new neighbors who moved into that house," Lily said.

Nick interrupted and asked Grandma if she had any newspaper clippings about the investigation.

"I think I might have kept some. Let me look in my attic. I'll be right back."

As the duo sat waiting, the reality of this case began to scare the detectives a little. A few moments later Grandma returned with a photo album. Inside were clippings of the entire investigation. There was a photo of the man that had been arrested.

Lily looked at Nick, and said, "That looks like the man we saw in the picture at Brianna's house."

Lily and Nick now knew the identity of the couple in the picture. They gave Grandma a big hug and left to continue on with their investigation.

"Now where do we go, Lily?" Nick asked.

"I think we need to go back to Brianna's house."

Nick thought for a while, and said, "We had better wait until tomorrow, because it's getting late."

"Okay, see you tomorrow."

Later that evening, Lily began having one of her dreams. This time she was in the house where the mother and son were allegedly killed. Lily heard voices coming from a room somewhere in the house. She walked around and finally found them in the kitchen. Lily quietly listened to the argument. It sounded like the mother and father were yelling about getting a divorce. The man was extremely angry and told her he would never get a divorce from his family. Suddenly, Lily felt something touch her arm. It was the son. Trying to be brave, Lily asked him what his name was. He said his name was James, but he liked to be called Jimmy. Lily asked Jimmy if his parents fought like this all of the time. Before he could answer, Lily woke up.

Sitting up in bed, Lily knew she had found an important clue in solving this mystery. She lay in bed and kept replaying her dream over and over in her head. What was the importance of this dream?

Lily tried to go back to sleep, but couldn't. She decided to get up and look at the photo album she had borrowed from her Grandma. Lily opened up to one article in the album. The column stated the man arrested denied killing his family and did not know what had happened to them. He said that when he left that night, both his son and wife were fine. He said they had had an argument about getting a divorce. The man said that during their argument he had cut himself on a broken cup. His wife told him to leave for a while to cool off, so he left. Once gone, he decided it would be best for his family if he never returned. His wife wanted a divorce, so he would set her free.

Lily put the album away to get some sleep. She wanted to be fully rested to continue with this investigation tomorrow.

The morning came quickly, and Lily was excited to get to Nick's house to fill him in on her dream. Lily knew Nick would not believe her dream, but that never stopped her from trying to convince him.

"Hi, Nick. I had a dream last night." Lily replied.

"What was it about this time?" Nick asked, trying to hide his disbelief.

Lily continued with her story. "I was inside the house when the man and his wife were arguing. They were fighting about getting a divorce. I even met the son. His name was Jimmy."

Nick looked at Lily, now totally convinced about her dream. "Lily, the name of your new neighbor is Jim Young. Do you think that he was the young boy you saw in your dream?"

Lily said, "I'm not sure. How can it be, the boy was supposedly killed by his father? I even read in one of my Grandma's newspapers that the man tried to tell the police and the judge that he didn't kill his family. He said that when he left, his wife and son were fine."

"Do you think all of that blood came from a cut on his hand?" Nick asked, more puzzled than ever.

Lily thought for a while, and said, "We need to find out the truth. Somebody's got to know more about this case."

Lily and Nick decided to ride over to Brianna's house to do some in-house investigating. Before arriving, Lily told Nick they couldn't tell Brianna about any of this yet. Brianna could not be fully trusted for now.

Nick and Lily arrived at Brianna's house to resume their investigation. Once inside, Lily asked Brianna if she had ever been in Scott City before.

"No, this is my first time to be in Kansas."

Lily continued questioning Brianna. "How about your parents, have they lived here before?"

Feeling confused, Brianna asked, "Why are you asking if we've lived here before?"

Nick quickly interrupted. "Oh, we're just curious, because we want to learn more about you and your family."

This eased Brianna's concern for the time being.

Lily did not want to stop questioning Brianna, so she decided to ask if she had a photo album they could look at.

Brianna went into the living room to retrieve the album. The new friends sat down on the sofa to look at the pictures.

As each page was being turned, Lily was carefully observing each photo, trying to find a picture of Brianna's dad when he was a child. Finally, toward the middle of the album, Lily saw the picture she was desperately searching for. "Who is this little boy?" Lily asked curiously.

"That's a picture of my dad when he was a child." Brianna said.

"Where did your dad grow up?" Nick asked.

Again feeling like she was being questioned too much, Brianna said, "I already told you, we are from Texas. He grew up in Waco, Texas!"

The duo knew she was getting upset by all of the questions and decided to change the subject.

Lily asked Brianna if she wanted to go ride around town on their bikes.

They took off for what they believed to be a short trip around town.

While off on their adventure, Lily suggested they go into the library to look at old newspapers.

"Why do you want to look at old papers for?' Brianna asked.

"I like looking in old newspapers to learn about the history of Scott City." Lily replied, hoping that Brianna would not question her anymore.

Lily searched the old papers for information about the case they were secretly investigating. Nick gave Lily a look to try to find out what on earth she was doing.

Lily whispered to her partner, "Don't worry, I'm being careful."

Lily found the newspaper she was looking for and laid it out on the table the new friends were sitting at. After flipping through the first couple of pages, Lily found an article about the death of the mother and son. She read it aloud, "The police were about to call the investigation of their deaths off, when they received an anonymous phone call telling them of the location of the father. The article continues by saying that the man was shortly arrested."

Brianna asked her new friends what all they knew of this story? Trying not to give away their investigation, Nick said that was the first time he'd heard of this story.

"Well, guys, it's getting late. The library's going to close soon. We need to get home," Lily said.

Nick and Lily helped Brianna find her way home before returning to Lily's house.

The trip to Lily's house went fast, since the detectives were anxious to talk about what they had learned today.

"Why did you bring Brianna to the library? I thought you were going to blow our case!" Nick scolded.

"I was trying to find out what she knew about this mystery. I needed to find out if we could trust her," Lily said.

"And what did you find out?" Nick asked.

"I think our new friend knows more about this case then she's letting on," Lily responded.

"Why do you think that?" Nick questioned his partner.

"Did you see the photo of her dad when he was a child?" Lily asked.

"Yes, so how does that help us?"

Lily continued. "Well, that was the little boy I saw in my dream," Lily said.

"So what do you think Brianna knows about this case?" Nick asked.

"The way she was asking what all we knew about this story led me to believe that she knows a lot more about this mystery than she's letting on," Lily replied.

The partners seemed to have run into a brick wall with no way out. All of the needed information was not coming together as it had on their previous case.

"Let's go back to my grandma's house. Maybe she knows someone who knew this family better than her," Lily said.

They needed some extra help and, hopefully, Grandma was the perfect candidate for the job.

Nick and Lily were feeling quite desperate, almost to the point of giving up on this new case.

Once they arrived at Grandma's house, the two seem to perk up when Grandma asked how their case was going.

"We need some help," Lily said.

"What kind of help?" Grandma asked. Before Lily could answer, Grandma handed the young detectives a small box.

"What's in this?" Nick asked.

"It's some of the family's belongings. I found them in their garage. The father left so fast that he must have forgotten about them. I'm not sure if this will help, but I saved it in case the police needed it for their investigation. They never did, so I guess you both can have it."

Lily opened the box and found a bundle of letters from someone.

Nick opened one of the envelopes and read:

Dear Jack,

> *I haven't heard from you and your family in several months. I hope all is well and I look forward to your visit in the summer. Please remind Joyce and Jimmy about bringing their swimsuits. We do plan on going swimming at the country club. Please write soon. I miss you all very much.*

Love, Mom \ Granny

"We now know all of their names. That can help us with finding them," Lily said.

"Better than that, we have their grandma's address. Look, she lives in Garden City, Kansas," Grandma said.

"Grandma, can you drive us to Garden City. We need to talk with her and see if she can answer some of our questions," Lily said, sounding like a private investigator.

"Well, first we need to call information and to make sure that she still lives there. Wait a minute and I'll call," Grandma said, trying not to get too excited.

As Lily and Nick waited, their minds raced with thoughts of how this case would turn out.

"Okay, kids. She still lives there and I called to let her know that we are on our way to visit her."

The three took a road trip to finally get the answers to all of these important questions.

The trip to Garden City seemed to take hours, but in actuality it only took half an hour. Eventually they arrived at the grandmother's house. The house was as big as a mansion.

"Boy, they must really be rich!" Nick said excitedly.

Lily rang the doorbell, and an old woman answered the door. "Hello Ma'am, my name is Lily, this is my grandma, Lillian, and this is my friend Nick." Lily said.

"Yes, welcome to my home. Won't you all come inside?"

The three slowly walked in, still marveling at how large the house truly was.

"I'm sorry to bother you, but I used to be neighbors with your son and his family," Grandma said.

"Ma'am, we are trying to find out what happened to your grandson and his mother," Lily said, trying to sound somewhat sensitive.

"Please call me Dorothy. I don't understand what you're saying. My son was arrested for their murder. Are you saying they are still alive?" Dorothy asked.

"We think that Lily's new neighbor may be your grandson Jimmy," Nick said.

"All of these years my son has been in prison for something he never did," Dorothy said as she sat down.

"Dorothy, I think with your help we can get him released from prison," Nick said gently.

"How can I help?" Dorothy asked.

"We need to get you back to Scott City, and I want you to meet Jim Young and see if he is truly your grandson," Lily replied.

The time had now come for Jim to come face to face with Dorothy. Hopefully, the two detectives were well on their way to solving another mystery.

Lily knocked at the Young's door and James came face to face with his past.

"Hello, do I know you?" he asked.

"Yes Jimmy, I'm your grandma," Dorothy said, with a tear in her eye.

James looked confused, and said, "My grandma died when I was just a toddler."

"No, I didn't. Who told you that?" Dorothy asked.

"My mom told me when we moved to Texas that she was the only family I had left," James said, trying hard to hold back a lifetime of tears.

"Jimmy did you know that your father has been in prison for supposedly killing you and your mother?" Dorothy said.

"Why did my mom lie to me?" James asked, barely able to speak.

"Your mother did what she thought was best for you and her safety. My son was very abusive to your mother and she tried to protect you from getting hurt by him."

The pieces of the puzzle were slowly coming together.

"How did you find me?" James asked.

"These two young detectives did the hard work. They actually tracked me down."

James got up and called Brianna into the living room. "Brianna, I want you to meet your grandma. She found us, thanks to your new friends."

She ran up to give her grandma a great big hug.

Before leaving, Lily said one final statement. "You need to contact the Scott City police department to let them know that you are still alive so they can get your father released from the state prison."

James looked at Nick and Lily, and said, "Don't worry; I'll take care of that work. Thanks for everything you have done for me and my family."

Nick and Lily left this newly reunited family to have some time to get to know each other.

"Well, Nick, looks like we've solved another mystery."

Before Nick could respond, Brianna came running up to them. "Thanks for being my friends. I'm sorry I seemed so private. I've never really had friends before. My family has moved around so much with my dad's job that I have never got to stay in one place for very long."

Both Lily and Nick said, "Its okay. We all need friends."

Even though this mystery was solved, Nick still had one final question to ask Brianna, "Why did your family move back into that house? I mean, that's the same house that your grandparents lived in."

Brianna said, "That house was donated to our family by the police department when we first arrived in town. It's hard to believe how that house remained in our family, even after all of this happened." Before riding off in search of another case, Brianna had one final thing to say to her friends. "The house really isn't haunted."

Nick asked, "How did you hear about that?"

"This isn't a very big city; word gets around fairly quickly," Brianna said.

Another one down, let's go find us another mystery to solve…

Chapter Three
The Stranger in the Lake

The detectives were really getting better at solving each of their mysteries. Lily and Nick knew that each mystery they found, the harder they were going to become to solve. Summer was flying by and the duo was starting to worry about having enough time to solve more cases before having to return to school.

Lily's family always went camping at the lake in Scott City, but this year she was allowed to invite a friend with her. Of course, she invited her best friend Nick. Lily packed all of her handy detective tools in her backpack, just in case a mystery needed to be solved.

Before leaving for the lake, Lily and Nick went back up to the secret tree to tell Michael Howard that they would not be able to visit him for a while. This made Michael a little sad, because they were his only friends. Lily promised that they would visit him just as soon as they arrived home from the lake.

Lily and Nick returned home just in time to jump into the van with Lily's family. The next mystery would soon present itself to these young sleuths.

The drive to the lake only took half an hour. Once they had arrived, they began to set up camp. While Lily's parents set up the tent, Nick and Lily went on a short walk. The walk into the woods could have been dangerous if they had not been paying attention to where they were going. Fortunately, Lily was a professional camper and knew to leave a trail of breadcrumbs just in case they did get lost.

"Lily, what kind of animals do you think live in the woods?" Nick asked.

"There are rabbits and squirrels," Lily said, not wanting to scare Nick.

"Don't you think there might be wolves and bears?" Nick kept probing Lily for the truth.

"Definitely not bears in Scott City, but there might be some wolves. The wolves are more scared of us then we are of them. Don't worry, we'll be fine. Remember, Nick, we have to find another case to solve."

As the two continued on with their walk, they kept a watchful eye for things that seemed odd.

After walking in the woods for about twenty minutes, they decided to go back to the campsite.

"Well, did you guys find anything interesting on your walk?' Dad asked.

"No," Lily and Nick said in unison.

"There's always tomorrow. Besides, I thought we'd stay up late and tell ghost stories. How does that sound?" Dad said eerily.

Everybody got washed up for dinner before it was time to settle in for some scary story time in the dark.

Now that everybody was full from eating and it was darker outside, it was time to begin telling the spooky ghost stories.

Dad began:

One cold summer day, way out far in the woods, a family decided to set up camp. In fact, this is the very same campsite that the family used. The father and son went out to go fishing at the lake. They sat at the edge of the water, just waiting for a huge fish to catch. They knew Mom was the best cook and the fish sure would taste good. The day passed by and nobody caught any fish. Just as they were about to leave, the son noticed something odd in the middle of the lake.

"Look, Dad, did you see that?"

The father, acting like his son was just teasing, said, "There's nothing out there. Stop before you make yourself scared."

The son, getting angrier as each second passed, finally said, "Dad, I'm not teasing. Just look out in the middle of the water!"

After a few more minutes went by, suddenly this large looking creature stood up from under the water and slowly walked over to the terrified family.

Dad screamed, "Run, son! Let's get back to the campsite and make sure Mom is okay."

They ran as fast as they possibly could, but directly behind them was this strange looking creature.

When the father and son arrived back at their campsite, they noticed that everything was shredded and couldn't find the mom anywhere.

Screaming at his son, the father yelled, "Get into the truck and lock the door." The dad tried to start the truck, but it wasn't working.

"Dad, what's going to happen to us? I'm so scared!"

Trying to calm his son down, the dad said, "It's alright, son, just keep your eyes closed very tight, and whatever happens don't open them!"

The creature was face to face with the terrified family. It kept banging on the truck and rocked it back and forth, back and forth.

"Dad, he's going to kill us!"

Dad continued saying, "Keep your eyes closed and don't look!"

Both the father and son sat extremely frightened, with their eyes closed, when all of a sudden it was quiet. After a few moments, they opened their eyes and discovered that the creature was gone.

"Dad, where did it go?" the son asked.

"It's gone, son. Let's get out of here before it returns," the father said.

"But what about Mom?" the terrified son asked.

"Don't worry, we'll go get help and they'll find Mom," the father said, trying to sound brave for his son.

When the father and son got back into town, they went straight to the police for help.

To this day nobody knows exactly what happened to the mother or has ever seen that creature again.

Lily and Nick were scared, but they both knew what their next case to solve would be. The creature in the lake would be a very exciting mystery to uncover.

Early the next morning, Lily and Nick decided to walk down to the lake to see if they might catch a glimpse of this lake monster. The lake seemed quite calm, without any sight of this unidentified creature. Nick and Lily decided to sit down at the edge of the water to wait and see if it would appear later.

Hours later, nothing had happened.

"Lily, do think that story your dad told was real?" Nick asked.

"The only way to find out is to investigate," Lily said.

The two detectives decided to walk around the edge of the lake in search of clues as to whether this creature really existed. Nick and Lily walked around the lake, but did not find one single clue leading to the identity of this creature.

"What do you think happened to the mother?" Nick asked as they were walking.

"I guess the creature killed her. It's just odd that the police never found any remains of her, or even something from the creature," Lily said, after thinking for a few moments. Lily knew there was more to this case then what they had heard from the story.

Lily and Nick decided to go back to Lily's dad to ask some important questions about this story.

Running back into the campsite, Lily asked her Dad, "Is that story you told us last night true?"

"I'm not sure. It's a story I was told when I was a young boy. Why do you ask?" Dad asked.

"We just thought we might do some investigating about this creature," Lily said, trying to sound like a professional detective.

"You both be careful. Make sure you stay fairly close. I want to be able to find you quickly."

Before leaving, Lily and Nick said, "Okay, we'll stay close."

The two detectives went on into the woods in order to do some investigating.

Lily and Nick walked quite a ways into the woods and didn't find any evidence of this monster.

"Nick, let's walk over to the mountain. I bet we might find something over there," Lily said.

"Alright, but what do you think we'll find?" Nick asked.

"I'm not sure, but anything is going to better than what we've found so far."

At the bottom of the mountain Lily found an opening to a cave. It appeared as though someone or something had been going in and out of it, because the grass growing in front of the opening was worn down.

"I'm scared Lily. Do you think the creature lives in there?" Nick asked.

"I don't know. Here, let's take our flashlights." Lily reached into her backpack. "Let's go."

Slowly walking into the cold, dark cave, Lily and Nick held hands. Once inside they noticed a strange smell.

"What's that smell?" Nick asked.

"I don't know. Let's keep looking."

As the duo continued on the walk into the cave, suddenly Lily heard a sound coming from the back of the cave.

"Lily, we need to get out of here! This is too dangerous," Nick said.

"Nick, it's alright. Just stay quiet. If we see anything, we'll run, okay?" Lily said calmly to her partner.

"Alright, but if I see that creature, I'm running out of here really fast!"

Walking slowly, their hearts racing faster than ever before, trying to not make any noise, the two sleuths saw something tall standing in the back of the cave. Not wanting to make any sudden movement, Lily very carefully shined her flashlight at it. The figure did not move.

"What is it?" Lily asked.

"I don't know, but whatever it is I don't think it's alive." Nick said.

Slowly they moved closer, closer, and even closer still. Then, face-to-face, the partners stood with this figure. Standing before them was not the creature, but was a huge mirror. The mirror had a painting of a creature on it.

"What is this? Why is there a picture painted on it?" Nick asked.

"This has to be a clue to the identity of the creature in the lake," Lily said.

Deciding it was getting late, they left to return to the campsite. Tomorrow they would return to this cave, but this time they would bring Lily's dad.

As they were walking up to the camp, Lily's mother rushed up to them. "Dad just left to look for both of you!" Mom shouted.

"I'm sorry, Mom. We lost track of time." Lily said, trying to sound sorry.

"Where have you guys been?" Mom asked.

"We found a cave back by the mountain," Nick said, before Lily could even speak.

"I hope you didn't go inside," Mom said.

"Well, we did, but we got scared and decided to leave and come back here," Lily said.

"I'm glad you're back. I don't want either of you to go back into that cave again. Do you understand?"

Lily and Nick both agreed, secretly knowing that this was a promise they wouldn't be able to keep.

A few minutes later, Dad returned. He saw that both of the children were safe and sound. Before he could even open his mouth to ask them where they had been…

"Dad, we found a cave. We think that's where the lake creature lives," Lily exclaimed.

"Honey, that creature doesn't exist. It's just a made up story," Dad said, trying not to laugh at them.

"You said yourself you weren't sure if it was real or not," Nick pleaded.

"I said that to scare you. I'm sorry. This creature was just made up; it's not real," Dad said, trying to convince both Lily and Nick.

"Dad, inside the cave we found this big mirror with a painting of a creature on it. We need you to come back with us tomorrow. Just see for yourself," Lily continued.

"Okay, we'll go back tomorrow morning. Promise me you won't go back in that cave without me," Dad said.

"We promise," Lily and Nick said in unison.

"Lily's mom told us not to go back in the cave. She made us promise," Nick said.

"Well, I won't tell her if you won't," Dad replied.

The investigation would continue tomorrow. This time they would bring reinforcements.

The next morning came, but before Lily and Nick could tell Mom they were going to go on a walk...

"Dad tells me you all are going on a walk into the woods," Mom said.

"Yes," Lily said, trying not to feel guilty for leaving her mom at the campsite alone.

Everyone ate their breakfast quickly in anticipation of what was waiting for them at the cave.

Once they were back at the cave, Lily took out her flashlights and handed them out.

"Listen, you guys stand behind me. Tell me, where did you see this mirror?" Dad asked.

"All the way toward the back of the cave," Lily said.

The three slowly walked deeper into the cave. When they arrived at the back of the cave, nothing was there. No mirror.

"I thought you said the mirror was here?" Dad asked.

"It was yesterday. It was right here!" Nick said, confused as to why it wasn't there.

"Are you sure we're in the right cave?" Dad asked.

"This is the only cave we found."

The three continued looking in the cave for any evidence of what Lily and Nick had found yesterday.

Lily got mad and sat down to think about what had happened to this mirror. As she did, she felt something cold under her hand. Lily shined her flashlight down on it and noticed it was an empty soda can. "Hey, look, guys, I found this here on the floor. Why do you think this would be in the cave?" Lily asked.

"Let me look at it," Dad said, carefully examining the empty can. Suddenly he noticed that this type of soda was no longer being made. "Well, whoever was in this cave is long gone. This soda hasn't been made for nearly ten years," Dad said.

"Why do you think anybody would be sitting in here drinking a soda?" Nick asked.

"That's a good question," Lily replied.

After looking around in the cave, the three decided there was nothing else to find. It was time to return back to the campsite. But before leaving the mountain, Lily and Nick wanted to look around the mountain, just in case they were in the wrong cave. Unfortunately, they didn't find any other caves. Lily and Nick were back to square one. Trying to identify this thing was going to be more difficult to solve than what they had initially anticipated.

The weekend at the lake went by fast, and now it was time to return home. While the campers were packing up all of their gear, a park ranger came up to the van to talk.

"Hi, folks. My name is Roy Tanner. Did you enjoy your time at my lake?" Roy asked.

"We sure did," Dad said.

Before he could continue talking with Roy, Lily interrupted and said, "Sir, have you heard the story of the lake creature?"

Roy grinned at her, and replied, "Well, honey, that's just a made up story to scare campers here at the lake."

Not allowing time for Lily to answer, Nick yelled, "No it's not! We found a cave, and inside we found a mirror with a picture of the creature painted on it."

"Have you seen this?" Roy asked Dad.

"We went up to the cave this morning…"

But, before he could continue, Mom interrupted, and said, "I told you both not to go in that cave anymore!"

Dad continued. "I'm sorry that's my fault. I told them I would go with them. Anyway, when we went into the cave, we couldn't find the mirror."

After thinking for a moment, Roy said, "Maybe you both were having so much fun exploring the cave that you got so excited that you simply pretended to see the mirror."

This type of talk always made Lily extremely mad. She didn't like it when adults treated her like a small child. "Sir, we didn't imagine seeing that mirror. It was there! "Lily yelled.

This conversation wasn't going the way the duo needed it to be going. The investigation would have to resume at home. Pretending that Roy was right, Lily and Nick agreed they had made up the entire adventure.

"You folks have a safe trip home and return to the lake again. It's nice having people out here," Roy said as everyone got into the van and headed back into town.

Right before leaving the lake, "Why did you take me to that cave if it wasn't real?" Dad asked.

"It was real. We just told him that because he didn't believe us," Lily said.

The investigation was not over yet.

Later that evening, Lily was tired and went to sleep early. She needed to get some rest in order to investigate this mystery tomorrow.

Lily's dreaming began instantly. Lily and Nick were back out at the lake, but this time they were watching the father and son fishing at the edge of the lake.

"Nick, let's go see what the mother is doing at the campsite."

They headed for the same campsite in which they had spent the last few days.

At first nothing seemed strange, but suddenly they heard a loud scream come from behind the bushes. Knowing that they could not be seen, Lily walked over to the bushes to have a peek.

"What do you see, Lily?"

"It looks like Michael Howard."

At that moment Lily woke up from this insightful dream.

Lying in bed reviewing this dream, Lily couldn't believe it. She kept questioning, *Why would Michael do something like that?* Lily was so awake and concerned, she decided to sneak out to Nick's house. She quietly got dressed and headed out the door to her partner's home.

Lily softly threw a couple of pebbles at Nick's bedroom window. It took a while for Nick to wake up and come to his window.

"Lily what are you doing? It's 2:00 in the morning. Why aren't you sleeping?"

"Nick I had a dream. Come down here. We need to talk."

Closing the window, Nick headed downstairs to talk with Lily. "Okay, tell me, what was it about this time?" Nick asked, half asleep.

"In this dream we were back at the lake and we saw the father and son fishing. We walked back to the campsite to check on the mother. We didn't see her, but suddenly we heard screams coming from behind the bushes," Lily said.

"And what was it?" Nick asked, interrupting his partner.

Lily took a deep breath, and said, "It was Michael Howard."

Not believing his ears, "What did you say? Did you say Michael Howard? Our friend?" Nick asked. "I know it's hard for me to believe too, but you know my dreams always are right. We need to go back to the tree to talk with Michael to see what he has to say about this," Lily said, trying to convince Nick that their friend could have killed this woman and scared the father and son.

"It's too early. Let's go back to sleep and tomorrow we'll go visit Michael. I'm tired and I want to go back to sleep," Nick said, hoping Lily would wait until later in the morning.

"Fine. I'll wait. See you at 8:00." Lily went back home to try to get some sleep, even though she knew it was useless.

Bright and early the next morning, Lily and Nick headed to their friend Michael's home in the tree.

While walking to the tree, "What do you think Michael will do when we ask him about this?" Lily asked.

"I hope he'll deny all of it and tell us that he didn't have anything to do with this family," Nick said.

Lily and Nick arrived at the tree and went inside. Once inside, they found Michael sitting in his room.

Seeing his friends, Michael got up to greet them. "Hello. How was your trip to the lake?" Michael asked.

"We discovered a new mystery," Lily said.

"What was it?" Michael asked.

Lily continued. "We heard about a family that found a strange creature in the lake. He killed the mother and chased the father and son away," Lily reported.

Michael looked at the two detectives, and asked, "Why are you telling me this?"

"Michael, I have dreams that tell me about things that have happened in the past. Anyway, in my dream last night, I saw you killing the mother. Michael, why would you do that?" Lily asked.

Michael didn't say anything. He just stood there and stared off into space.

"Michael, why won't you answer my question?" Lily asked, more firmly this time.

Still no response. Michael kept staring off into nowhere.

"Lily something's wrong with him."

Finally, after a while Michael broke his silence. "That was a long time ago. Before I learned who I was. That was a time in my life when I was an evil Taemite," Michael finally admitted.

"So it's true?" Nick asked.

"Yes, it's true."

Lily couldn't believe what her ears were hearing.

"So it really was you that killed that woman and scared the father and son. I don't understand, why did you kill the mother? She wasn't hurting you. Was she?" Nick asked.

Michael was feeling ashamed of what he'd done in the past. "I did what I was taught to do. I killed to be able to survive. When I learned who I was, I felt horrible for all of my past mistakes. I still go back up to the lake when it's late at night so nobody sees me. I found a cave that I stay in to think about what I've done to so many people," Michael said, reliving this horrible event from his past.

"So it was you that put the mirror in the cave?" Lily asked, still working on solving this new case.

"Yes, it was me. I did that when I was lonely. It made me feel like I wasn't alone anymore," Michael said.

"When we were at the lake, we went into your cave and found the mirror, but when we brought my Dad back to see it, it was gone." Lily said.

"Why did you move the mirror?" Nick asked, feeling like this mystery was slowly coming together.

Trying not to disappoint his friends, Michael said, "I didn't want your father or anybody to find out about me. I don't feel lonely anymore now that you are both my friends."

Lily, wanting to end this case, said, "You know, Michael, there's a story that's being told to campers late at night. This story tells how you attacked this family and killed the mother. You are a spooky tale being told to children in order to scare them," Lily said.

This case was now solved, but before leaving, Nick said, "Michael, we'll put an end to that story once and for all."

"You know, Michael, I think it's time you come out into the public. I know my family will help you, that way you can come over to our houses whenever you want."

Michael lowered his head, and said, "I love both of you very much, but other people would be scared of me. I would even be locked away because I killed people. I'm sorry, but I have to stay here. It's not bad anymore. I have friends now," Michael said.

Before leaving, Lily and Nick gave Michael a huge hug and left for home. It was time to spread the word around town that the story of the Lake Creature was not real.

Lily and Nick went home to bring a conclusion to this case once and for all. Lily and Nick were ready to begin looking for the next case to solve.

Chapter Four
The Party

Lily and Nick worked hard getting the word spread that the story of the creature in the lake was not true. That case was officially closed, and now it was time to search for the next. The summer was going by fast and the duo needed to find another mystery before it was time to return to school.

The days in July were extremely hot, especially in Scott City. The only way to get relief was by going to the local swimming pool. Unfortunately, everybody else had the same idea. The pool was crowded and someone was always bumping into you.

One hot, sunny day Lily and Nick were enjoying spending time playing in the pool. Nick was known for his B-1 belly bombers into the pool. Interrupting their fun, they saw Kristina Lewis walking straight up to them.

Kristina was the one person that drove Lily absolutely crazy. Ever since they were in the second grade, Kristina constantly made fun of the way Lily dressed. To this day, Lily made sure she avoided her at all times. Everyone in town knew that Kristina's family was extremely wealthy, and the family always made sure that everybody knew it.

"Hi, guys. Bet you can't guess what my daddy's made me?"

Trying to avoid a fistfight, Nick asked, "What is it?"

Smiling her usual snobbish smile, Kristina said, "A huge swimming pool! Now I won't have to worry about swimming with you local people."

Before Lily could make a comment back in reply, Nick said, "That sounds wonderful."

Once Kristina shared her news, she was off to brag to the next group of people.

Trying to cheer Lily up, Nick said, "Do you want a Popsicle? I'm buying."

Lily perked up, and said, "If you're buying, I'll take a cherry one. Thanks."

As Nick walked over to the concession stand, Lily sat at the edge of the pool trying to forget about Kristina.

Nick sat down beside Lily and the two of them enjoyed their refreshing treats.

The day quickly went by, so the detectives left to get home before their parents got worried about them.

"Thanks for cheering me up. You know you are my best friend!" Lily said.

"You're mine too! See you tomorrow," Nick replied.

That evening Lily was a little sad. Just thinking about how Kristina treated her made Lily's blood boil. She decided that some day Kristina would get what was coming to her, but for now she would just have to wait.

Eventually Lily fell asleep and, like many other nights, she began having one of her dreams. This dream began with Lily in school. Nothing seemed weird at first. Lily was sitting in her history class waiting for the teacher to arrive to start class. As she was sitting there, she wondered where Nick was, because he normally sat right beside her. Lily got up to go check in the hall for Nick, and suddenly everybody was laughing and pointing at her. She looked down and noticed she was in her pajamas. Lily ran out the door feeling completely humiliated. Right before she reached the girls locker room, she heard some muffled voices at the other end of the hall. Lily quietly walked over to where the voices were coming from and saw her worst fear come true. Kristina and Nick were kissing. Lily let out a loud gasp, then Kristina noticed that Lily had seen them. Kristina and Nick started laughing at Lily. Feeling brokenhearted, Lily took off running down the hall.

All at once Lily was back in her bed. She sat up and tried to figure out why she had that horrible dream. Knowing that her dreams were never wrong, Lily felt as though her friendship with Nick was about to come to an end.

Lily tried to get some sleep, but her mind kept replaying the dream. How could Nick allow something like that to happen? He knew how much I couldn't stand Kristina.

Morning finally came, so Lily left for Nick's house. Her mind wondered what Nick's reactions would be. Hopefully, Nick could help her feel better, because this was a time she desperately needed her best friend.

Lily arrived at Nick's house and noticed he was sitting on his porch reading a card.

"Hi, Nick, what are you reading?" Lily asked.

"Oh, it's nothing. Why are you here so early?" Nick asked.

"I had a dream and needed to talk to you," Lily said softly, trying to warn Nick about how upset she actually was.

"What was it about?" Nick asked.

"I was in sitting in history class waiting for our teacher to arrive…"

Not letting Lily continue her story, Nick asked, "What's so weird about that?"

Lily tried to remain calm, so she said, "Anyway, I noticed you weren't in class, so I got up to go look for you in the hall. As I stood up, everyone started pointing at me and laughing. I ran out to go to the girls locker room. As I reached the locker room, I heard voices coming down from the hall, so I quietly walked down to where the voices were coming from and suddenly I saw you kissing Kristina. You both started laughing at me. That's when I woke up. So what do you have to say about that?" Lily asked, hoping Nick would say what she desperately wanted to hear.

Nick sat there not knowing what to say, then very caring, Nick said, "You know, Lily, sometimes your dreams won't come true. This is one I am strongly guaranteeing will not come true."

Lily was starting to feel better. "But what if she really likes you? Even though I can't stand her, she still is a very pretty girl and she's rich." Lily asked.

"Lily, I promise you, I don't think of Kristina like that. My best friend doesn't like her, so I don't like her. That's the end of the story!" Nick said.

Nick had made Lily feel a lot better, so the duo decided to go ride their bikes around town.

During their trip through town, Lily and Nick decided to go into MacDonald's for a soda. While they were sitting at a table, a couple of kids from school came walking up to them.

"Hi, guys. We got our invitations to go to the swimming party. Did you get yours?" Loresa asked.

"What invitation?" Lily asked.

"To go to Kristina's 'End of the Summer' party. She only invited certain people." Loresa said.

Lily looked at Nick. "Was that what you were reading this morning?" Lily asked.

"Yes, but I wasn't going to go. I'm sorry, Lily, I didn't want you to hear about it."

Before Nick could continue his conversation with Lily, Loresa said, "I guess that means that Lily didn't get an invitation to the party," as she walked away, laughing at how happy she was that Lily wasn't invited.

Lily was beginning to feel like she did when she was in grade school all over again.

"Don't listen to her, she's a jerk!" Nick said, trying to get Lily to forget about all of this nonsense.

"You know what, Nick? I think you should go to the party. Maybe we could get even with Kristina," Lily said.

"How would we do that?" Nick asked.

"I don't know yet, but just wait, it'll come to me!"

Lily and Nick got back on their bikes to continue on with their ride.

While riding, it finally came to Lily, she had the perfect idea. "I've got it!" Lily shouted.

"What is it?" Nick asked.

"Go to the party and act like we had a huge fight. Pretend like we aren't friends anymore and you want to become good friends with her."

Nick thought about it for a while, then asked, "How we are going to get even with Kristina?"

The wheels in Lily's head were turning quickly; she tried not to talk too fast, so she continued. "By you pretending to be her friend, we can figure out why she is so mean to me," Lily said.

"Okay, but I'm not so sure that this is such a good idea. I don't want to hurt her or anybody," Nick said.

"Don't worry, we are just going to investigate why Kristina is the way she is."

Lily and Nick continued going over different ways they could convince Kristina that Nick wanted to become her close friend.

"The only way this can happen is if you try to get her to kiss you. Just like my dream," Lily said.

"What? No, I already said I didn't like her that way. Besides, I don't want to hurt her feelings," Nick said, trying to convince Lily.

"Nick, I know that, but remember I have my dreams for a reason. My dream was showing me how to solve the mystery of Kristina."

Finally Nick agreed to the plot and the duo left to return home.

This case was going to be harder than any of the others.

The day of the swimming party arrived. Although Nick was still unsure of this plan, he went ahead and left for Kristina's house.

Nick got to Kristina's party a little early, just so he could have some alone time with her. Nick rang the doorbell. After a few moments Kristina came to the door.

"I didn't think you were going to come," Kristina said.

"Me and Lily got into a big fight about you." Nick tried to sound convincing.

"Over me? Now why would you get into an argument over me?" Kristina asked.

"Lily thinks that I can't be friends with you. She told me if I went to your party, then we wouldn't be friends anymore," Nick said.

"You and Lily aren't friends anymore?" Kristina asked.

"No. So why don't you show me around your house. I've never been here before," Nick said.

"Sure."

As they walked into Kristina's house, she reached over and took his hand, and said, "It's alright, Nick. I'll be your new friend."

This really made Nick feel uneasy, but he said, "That would be great!"

The new friends spent time talking about their families. Eventually, Kristina asked. "Do you have a girlfriend?"

Nick took a gulp, and said, "No."

This gave Kristina the chance to tell Nick that she had had a huge crush on him since they were in grade school.

"Why didn't you tell me before?" Nick asked.

"I know it's hard to believe, but I have never had a boyfriend," Kristina said.

"You were just waiting for me to come along. Weren't you?" Nick asked teasing.

"Yes, I was," Kristina said.

"There's one thing that I really want to know," Nick asked.

"What?" Kristina asked.

"Why are you so mean to Lily? I mean, she never did anything to you."

Kristina looked directly in Nick's eyes, and said, "I have always been jealous of Lily. I mean, she always had you right there beside her. I wanted you to be with me, not her," Kristina admitted.

Others began arriving for the party, so Nick and Kristina decided to go out to the pool. Everyone at the party seemed surprised that Nick had come, and even more surprised by the fact that Nick and Kristina were holding hands. Nick knew that the plan had worked. He now had Kristina right where they needed her to be. Next step was to fill Lily in on how successful the plan had worked.

Bright and early the next morning, Nick rode over to Lily's house. Much to his surprise, Lily was sitting on the porch waiting for him.

"Hi. How was the party?" Lily asked.

"I wasn't so sure that Kristina would fall for it, but she did," Nick said.

"Tell me everything!" Lily said.

"She talked about how she has had a crush on me since she was in grade school. I asked her why she was always so mean to you." But, before he could continue...

"What did she say?" Lily asked.

"As I was trying to say before you interrupted, she told me she was jealous of you," Nick said.

"Why on earth would she be jealous of me?' Lily asked.

"She said because I spend all my time with you. She thinks we aren't friends anymore and now everyone thinks that me and Kristina are dating," Nick said, sounding disappointed in himself.

"She definitely fell into our trap," Lily happily said.

"Yes. Now what do we do?" Nick asked, although he already knew the answer.

"You have to pretend like you are her boyfriend and uncover a deep, dark secret about her. Something that we can use to get even with her," Lily said, trying to control her excitement.

"Lily, I don't think that's a nice thing to do, even for someone as mean as Kristina," Nick said, hoping that would convince his friend not to continue on with the plan.

"Today you need to go back to Kristina's house, and I'll go with you. You keep her distracted so I can sneak inside and do some private investigating," Lily said.

"Alright, let's go," Nick said.

While Nick ran the doorbell, Lily went to hide in a bush by the swimming pool. Once inside, Nick asked, "Kristina, can we go sit by the pool?"

"Sure. Do you want something to drink?" Kristina asked.

"Whatever you're having is fine with me," Nick said before going outside to warn Lily.

Kristina brought out two glasses of tea and sat down beside Nick on the lawn chair.

"Thanks. That sure tastes good!" Nick said. Knowing that he had to distract Kristina long enough to allow Lily time to sneak inside, he leaned in to give Kristina a kiss.

While her best friend was kissing her worst enemy, Lily dashed past them and went into the house. Inside the house, Lily quickly went upstairs to find Kristina's room. There were so many rooms that it took a while to find it.

Finally Lily found Kristina's bedroom and went inside. She noticed that it was a huge room. Even though Lily hated Kristina, she had to admit that she did have good taste in her choice of decorating.

Lily began searching for Kristina's diary. "Now where would you put your most treasured possession?" Lily asked herself. Realizing that the diary would be hidden from plain sight, Lily searched under Kristina's private belongings. Lily went over to her closet and saw a box full of stuffed toys and in the bottom of the box was her diary. Lily quickly put it in her backpack and very quietly snuck out of the house. Before leaving, Lily got Nick's attention by making a sound like a bird.

"Excuse me, Kristina, I need to run inside to go to the bathroom," Nick said politely, as he quickly walked down a hallway to find his partner.

"I found it! Make up an excuse and meet me at my house in five minutes," Lily ordered.

As Nick was about to return to the pool, Kristina came inside to check on what was taking him so long.

"Hey what happened to you, Nick?" Kristina asked.

"Oh, I'm sorry, but I just remembered I have to meet my mom for an appointment," Nick said.

"What kind of appointment?" Kristina asked.

"I have to go to the dentist for a checkup," Nick said.

"Okay, will I see you tomorrow?" Kristina asked.

"Sure, see you then," Nick said as he eagerly left.

Nick quickly rode over to Lily's house to see what she had found.

"Well, it sure took you long enough," Lily said.

"I tried to leave as fast as I could," Nick said.

"I found Kristina's diary. I bet there is a lot of juicy information in here!" Lily said.

"Go ahead and read it aloud," Nick said.

"Let's start toward the front. It says that on April 20 she was called to the principal's office. When she entered the office, she noticed her Mom was there crying. *Not knowing what was wrong; I bent down to Mom's side to ask her what was wrong? She looked at me and said that they had received a letter from an attorney.* The letter said that Kristina's birth mom wanted her back."

Nick looked at Lily, and said, "Did you know she was adopted?"

"No, I didn't. I guess that something that nobody here knows about," Lily said. Lily resumed reading Kristina's diary. "It says, later that evening, Kristina and her parents met with their attorney and learned that, according to the law, Kristina would have to return to her biological mother."

Lily and Nick were stunned by what they read in Kristina's diary.

"So what are we going to do with this information?" Nick asked.

"I feel sorry for her. You know what, I don't want to get even with her anymore. I think we need to help Kristina. I know I wouldn't want to leave my family," Lily said.

Although Lily at one time felt nothing but anger toward Kristina, now she only felt pity.

"Does it say when she has to leave?" Nick asked.

"Yes, Kristina has to return to her birth mother on August 30," Lily read.

"Where does her birth mother live?" Nick asked.

"She lives right here in Scott City." Lily informed her partner.

After thinking for a moment, Lily had another bright idea. "Instead of investigating why Kristina is so mean, I think we need to convince her birth mother to leave her with her adopted parents."

The duo had changed their plans and now was eager to help their classmate.

"How can we do that?" Nick asked.

"We need to come clean with Kristina and tell her everything," Lily said.

"What do you mean?' Nick asked, already knowing what Lily was thinking.

"I mean everything. She needs to know so she can trust us," Lily said.

"Okay, let's go."

Nick and Lily got on their bikes to ride over to Kristina's house to confess what they had planned to do to her.

Nick rang the doorbell, and shortly Kristina came to the door.

"Hi, Nick. What are you doing here, Lily?" Kristina asked.

"Listen, we need to tell you something," Nick said.

"Okay, go ahead."

They walked inside and sat down in the living room.

"Kristina, first of all, let me say I really like you. When I came to the party, I had an ulterior motive. We wanted to get something juicy on you so we could get even with you because you are so mean to Lily." Nick tried to sound sympathetic.

"So I guess you found it then."

Lily looked at Kristina, and said, "Yes, but I didn't want it to turn out like this."

Kristina was beginning to feel worried. "What did you find?" Kristina asked.

"We found out that you have to return to live with your birth mother," Nick said tenderly.

"How did you find that out?" Kristina asked.

Lily interrupted, and said, "It's not important. We want to help you stay with your family."

Trying not to cry, Kristina asked, "How can you guys do that?"

"We are going to talk with your birth mother and convince her to leave you alone," Nick said.

"Why do you want to help me?" Kristina asked.

"Because we want to be your friends," Lily said.

Now that the confession was complete, it was time to figure out how to convince Kristina's birth mother to leave her alone.

The day was passing quickly and the three friends still had no idea how to help Kristina.

"Do you have her address?" Lily asked.

"Yes, my mom has all of that information on her desk in the den," Kristina replied.

"I think we need to go directly to her house and just tell her how you feel about all of this," Lily said.

"I'm not so sure that I'm ready to come face to face with her," Kristina said.

Nick grabbed Kristina's hand, and said, "Its okay, Kristina, you've got me and Lily as your friends now. We'll be right beside you."

Feeling not so sure about the plan, Kristina agreed and the three new friends left to go to Kristina's birth mother house.

The friends got on their bicycles and left to meet the stranger that was causing so much pain to Kristina and her family.

During the ride, Kristina began picturing what type of person her birth mother was. She envisioned her as a poor, sickly woman living in an old rundown shack. Finally the moment arrived, the new friends were about to come face to face with Kristina's birth mother.

The house was not a shack at all. In fact, it was a fairly nice house. Not as big and fancy as Kristina's house, but still a very modest house just the same.

Lily rang the doorbell.

Nick noticed Kristina seemed very scared. He grabbed her hand. "It's going to be alright. We are here to help you," Nick said tenderly.

Not saying anything, Kristina simply nodded her head.

The door slowly opened. Standing right before their eyes was a young child. She looked exactly like Kristina had when she was that age.

Lily quickly asked, "Is your mommy home?"

The young girl nodded her head and left.

A few moments later a woman came to the door. Without having to introduce themselves, the woman said, "Kristina, is that you?"

The tears began flowing down Kristina's cheeks.

Trying to break the tension, Nick said, "Could we come inside?"

They went inside and sat down to talk with this stranger.

Knowing that Kristina was in no shape to question the motives of this woman, Lily decided to begin the investigation herself. "My name is Lily and this is my friend, Nick. We are here to help our friend convince you to leave her with her family."

The woman smiled. "Well, my name is Nancy. You met your sister, Cami. The reason I want you back is because I love you and you are my child," Nancy said.

Feeling overwhelmed, Kristina asked, "How can you say that. You gave me up for adoption. You had your chance with me and you chose to leave me."

Nick knew that this conversation was about to get heated. "Ma'am we only want what's best for Kristina. She loves her family and they love her."

Nancy stood up and said, "Where are my manners? Let me get us something to drink. I'll be right back."

The second Nancy left the room, Lily asked Kristina, "Are you alright?"

Kristina was no longer sad. In fact, she was angry. "I am so mad. How dare she think that she can just come back into my life and pretend that none of this ever happened!" Kristina yelled.

Nancy returned with a tray of lemonade and cookies. They quietly drank the lemonade. The time had now arrived to reveal the hidden secrets of Kristina's past.

Nancy began. "Kristina, when I first moved to Scott City I didn't know anyone. I got a job at your father's law office. He was always so kind to me. Joe made sure that if I ever needed anything; all I had to do was to ask him. As the years progressed, our friendship soon turned into love. Joe was always honest with me. He told me from the beginning that he was not going to leave his wife. That didn't matter to me. I loved just being with him, even if it meant only for a short while. Eventually I became pregnant. When I told Joe, he was angry at first, but he soon told me that he would send me to his vacation house in Denver while I had the baby. Joe convinced me that I would not be able to take care of you. He went to his wife and told her of his infidelity. Joe's wife was such a caring woman that she told Joe that the two of them would adopt you. Nobody ever needed to learn about this indiscretion."

All of this information was whirling in Kristina's head. "You mean, my parents kept this secret from me all of these years?"

With tears flowing down her face, Nancy continued. "Honey, we did what we thought would be the best for you. But you have to know, right after I signed the adoption papers I changed my mind and I wanted you back. Your parents have a lot of money and even more connections in this town. I tried everything I knew, but I couldn't get you back," Nancy said, with tears flowing down her face.

Nick and Lily looked at each other.

"Then how is it that Kristina has to leave them to come and live here with you?" Lily asked.

"Two years ago, Joe came to see me. He came to try to convince me to drop this; that it would be better for you to remain with them. The moment he came into my home, my old feelings for your father returned. I reached to touch his hand, and when I did Joe reached over and kissed me. Our relationship was not over like I had thought. I loved your father so much. I pleaded with him to leave your mother and marry me. Although I already knew what his answer was going to be, I continued pleading with him. Joe once more told me that he would not leave his wife. Joe left me brokenhearted as always.

I later learned I was pregnant again. There was no doubt in my mind; the baby was Joe's. I called Joe to inform him of my circumstances. He yelled at me for setting him up. Before I left your father's office, I told him that I was keeping this baby and I was going to fight to get you back."

Kristina was speechless, but somehow managed to ask, "Does my mom know about my sister?"

' Without saying a word, Nancy nodded.

Lily knew that Kristina needed time to come to terms with all of this, so she said, "Nancy, thanks for taking the time to talk with us. We need to leave, but we'll be back."

The three friends left the house not knowing what needed to be done next.

Once outside, Kristina said, "Thanks for coming with me. I couldn't have done that without both of you. I need to go home." It was time for Kristina to confront her parents.

"Do you want us to go with you?" Nick asked.

"No, I think I have to do this by myself. I'll call you when I'm done."

The three friends parted ways.

Kristina arrived home and went straight into her father's office. Much to her surprise, both her parents were inside.

"Mom, Dad, I have something I need to ask you."

Knowing her daughter was upset, Judy asked, "What's wrong, honey?"

Taking a deep breath, Kristina began. "I met Nancy today. She told me everything. Why would you lie to me?"

Joe and Judy looked quite upset.

"We did what was best for you. Nancy was young and wasn't financially able to care for you. Your mom was not able to have children, so we decided that this was the best solution," Joe pleaded.

Kristina continued drilling for answers. "If that's the truth, why then would you resume the affair with Nancy?"

Joe took another deep breath. "Honey, love is a mysterious thing. You don't get to choose who you fall in love with. I knew it was wrong, but a part of me still loved Nancy. I was weak and gave into temptation. I went straight home and told your mom. Once Nancy told me she was pregnant again, we knew that our family was not going to be the same ever again," Joe confessed.

Kristina's life was completely changing and she felt helpless. She ran upstairs to her room and locked the door. Kristina picked up her phone to call Nick.

Nick answered the phone instantly, hoping it was Kristina.
"Hi, Nick, this is Kristina," she said.
"Well, how did it go?" Nick asked.
"Everything Nancy told us is true. Oh, Nick, what's going to happen to me?" Kristina said, trying not to cry. "I love my mom and dad. I don't want to live with Nancy. I know she's a nice woman, but she's a stranger to me," Kristina cried.

"Kristina, you don't have to do anything right now. Let me and Lily see what we can do to help you," Nick said softly.

"Nick why are you and Lily being so nice to me? I've been so mean to Lily," Kristina asked.

"Don't worry about the past. Everybody makes mistakes. We are friends now. Anyway, let us help you. I'll go over to Lily's house and see what we can do to help. I'll talk to you soon, and remember, you aren't alone; you have me and Lily with you now," Nick said.

Nick hopped on his bike to ride over to Lily's house.

Lily was sitting on her porch.
"Hey, Lily, I just got off the phone with Kristina. Everything Nancy said was true."

Lily just sat there shaking her head in disbelief.

Nick continued on. "We have to help her, Lily."

"How are we supposed to do that?" Lily asked.

The duo sat and tried to figure out how to rescue Kristina from this life-changing event.

"Well, it's getting late. Come back over tomorrow morning and hopefully we'll have some ideas by then," Lily told her partner in crime.

"Okay, see you in the morning," Nick said in reply.

Lily lay on her bed and said, "Okay, Lily, now is the time I need some answers. Dreams, come to me and show me the way."

Sleep came quickly as it always had, and before long Lily was sitting in her grandma's house having milk and cookies.

"Lily, what's wrong? You look so sad," Grandma asked.

"My friend Kristina just found out she is adopted and now her birth mother wants her back."

Trying to come up with just the right words to say, Grandma softly said, "Sweetie, people make mistakes in life. I'm sure Kristina's birth mother loves her dearly and regrets making the mistake of letting her baby go to another couple."

Lily interrupted, and said, "That's just it, Grandma, Kristina's dad had an affair with her birth mother and then her parents raised Kristina as their own."

"Oh, I see. You know, honey, there's an answer to this dilemma."

Lily looked excitedly at her Grandma, and asked, "What is it?"

"There are many families that have joint custody of their children. I think that the answer to this problem is simply let Kristina remain living with her parents and visit with her birth mother until they become comfortable around each other. Once they feel like mother and daughter, then Kristina can spend more time at her birth mother's house; maybe even spend weekends there. In time, this new arrangement will not seem so bad." Grandma said.

"That's it! I can't believe the answer was that easy! Grandma, thanks so much!"

Lily sat up in bed, feeling relieved that she had the answer to help her new friend, Kristina.

The next day Lily got on her bike and rode quickly over to Nick's house. Lily pounded on Nick's bedroom window, frantically trying to wake him up.

"Lily, I was sleeping. What's wrong?" Nick asked, rubbing the sleep from his eyes.

"I had a dream. I know how we can help Kristina. Go and get dressed and meet me outside. Make it quick! We have a lot of work to do." Lily went up to the porch to wait impatiently for Nick.

After what seemed like eternity, Nick finally came outside. "Okay, what's your idea?"

Lily preceded telling Nick about her dream. "Last night, in my dream, my grandma told me that with both families sharing custody, Kristina's life wouldn't have to totally change. I just hope we can convince everyone that this will work."

Nick thought for a few moments, and finally said, "You know what, Lily, I think that just might work. We better go see Kristina and tell her about this idea."

"No, I don't think we need to tell Kristina just yet. Let's not say anything until we know this will work. She's already been through enough."

"Okay, that's probably a good idea. Well then, let's go," Nick said.

The duo rode off to go to Nancy's house to try to convince her of this perfect solution.

Lily and Nick arrived at Nancy's house and quickly rang the doorbell.

"Well, what a surprise. What are you two doing here?" motioning Nick and Lily inside.

Lily began. "I know you love Kristina a great deal, but you have to understand that you are asking her to walk away from the only family she's ever known."

Nancy added, "I don't want to hurt my baby, but I made a mistake by letting her go and now I want to correct that error."

Lily continued. "I know, but I think I have the perfect solution. Why don't you and Mr. And Mrs. Lewis share joint custody? That way it will give you and Kristina time to get to know each other."

Nancy sat quietly thinking for a while, and said, "If that will get me back in Kristina's life, then I'll do it. But what about Joe and Judy, will they be okay with this arrangement?" Nancy asked.

"There's only one way to find out. Let's go over to their house and ask them," Nick replied.

The three got into Nancy's car and drove over to Kristina's house.

During the drive, Lily asked, "Does your younger daughter know that Joe is her father also?"

"Cami doesn't know anything about her father. She's so young and doesn't understand any of this." Nancy said.

"Well, I think it's time this whole family becomes united." Lily replied.

"One step at a time, okay?" Nancy said.

They shortly arrived at Kristina's house and rang the doorbell.

Much to everyone's surprise, Kristina answered the door. "Nancy, what are you doing here?"

"May we come inside, honey?"

Kristina brought everyone into the living room.

"Are your mom and dad home?" Nick asked.

"Yes, I'll go and get them." Kristina quietly left to find her parents.

After a few minutes, Kristina returned with her parents.

"Hi, Lily and Nick. Well, Nancy, why are you here? Do we need to call our attorney?"

Lily intervened, and said, "No, Mr. Lewis. We have a solution to this problem. Nancy is willing to share joint custody with both of her children. This will give Kristina time to become acquainted with her birth mother. What do you think about that idea?"

Before Mr. Lewis could respond, Kristina said, "I would like to try it for a while, just to see. Is that okay?" Kristina looked lovingly at all of her family.

"Yes, Kristina, if that's what you want, then we'll give it a try." Mrs. Lewis responded.

Kristina walked over to Nancy and gave her biological mother their first hug.

Lily and Nick quietly got up to leave this newly reunited family alone.

Kristina ran out after them, and said, "Guys, I don't think I can ever thank you enough."

Lily replied, "Just be our friend, that's all we want."

Kristina gave Nick and Lily a great big hug. Kristina now had two new best friends.

Chapter Five
The Land of Strapron

Lily sat up in bed and suddenly realized that in just one short week school would be back in session. Feeling like the summer had just flown by, she threw her blankets over her head trying to escape this undeniable reality. Just as she had convinced herself that she could simply hide under her blankets and escape the torture of having to go back to school, her mother yelled for her to come downstairs and eat breakfast. They were going to go shopping for school supplies.

As slowly as humanly possible, Lily got dressed and went to have breakfast.

"Honey, aren't you excited about returning to school?" Mom asked.

"I can't solve any cases at school!" Lily responded.

"It's alright if you want to become a private investigator, but you know you have to go to school to actually become one. Besides, there might be a mystery to solve at school," Mom said as she rolled her eyes.

Lily had heard all of this before. "You never know what's going to happen," Lily said. She quickly ate breakfast and asked her mom, "When we're done, can I go over to Nick's house?"

"I guess that's alright."

Lily is not a girl that enjoyed going shopping for anything, but after seeing what Kristina had been through last week, Lily knew that it would make her mom happy, so she endured the hours of agony spent shopping.

Finally they were done and Lily was free to go visit her partner in crime, Nick.

Lily arrived at Nick's house and found him sitting on the front porch. "Hey, Nick, what's wrong? You look upset." Lily asked.

"I'm just bummed that summer's almost over. Aren't you?" Nick asked.

"Of course I am, but there's nothing that can be done. Anyway, I don't want to waste our last few days moping around not doing anything. Do you?" Lily asked.

"No. Hey, do you want to go and visit Michael? We haven't visited him for quite a while," Nick asked.

"Yeah, let's go. This will probably be our last time to see him until winter recess," Lily said.

The duo jumped on their bikes and rode off to the hidden tree.

While riding to the junkyard, Lily asked, "Nick, do you think we'll find a real case to solve at school this year?"

"We can always look. You know, Lily, you always seem to find a mystery anywhere you go," Nick said, trying not to sound doubtful.

Finally they arrived at the junkyard and walked into the woods to find Michael. The trip into the woods seemed to get quicker now that they were more familiar with the area.

Once inside the tree, they called out for Michael, but he didn't answer them.

"Where do you think he is?" Nick asked.

"I'm not sure. It's not like Michael to leave the tree during the day. Let's go and see if he's in his room," Lily added.

Nick and Lily walked through the magical tree. No longer were they scared of the magical powers that were hidden throughout this peculiar tree.

When inside Michael's bedroom, Lily saw something that actually took her breath away. "Hey Nick, look!"

Running quickly to the aide of his friend, Nick said, "What happened?"

Trying to remain calm, Lily softly said, "Look on Michael's desk."

Nick looked, and said, "What is it?"

Lily very carefully reached her hand to pick up the strange object, and said, "I think it must be something that the Taemites used during their mysterious rituals. We really need to find Michael and ask him about it."

The duo knew that they needed to desperately find their secret friend and make sure he was all right.

"Let's look in here first, maybe he's busy in one of the other rooms," Lily ordered.

Each of the rooms was full of relics from the extinct Taemites. One room in particular seemed to stand out above all of the others. Lily and Nick decided that this room had to be an important clue in trying to locate their missing friend. The detectives began their investigation in this one room.

"Lily, look at this!" Nick yelled at his partner.

"Let me see it." Lily grabbed the long, silver object. She began searching this item, hoping that whatever it was used for would become evident to her. Lily eyed the strange object, and after a few minutes she pointed it at a chair that was directly beside Nick. Just as Lily was about to throw it down—BOOM!

"What did you do?" Nick asked.

After the smoke cleared the room, Nick noticed that the chair was no longer in the room. "Hey, Lily, look the chair is gone. Where did it go to?' Nick asked.

Lily once again looked at the silver object, then pointed it at the wall. BOOM! Again there was another loud explosion. Except this time, after the smoke cleared the room, the chair had returned and Michael was sitting on it.

"Michael where have you been?" Lily asked.

"I've been visiting my new friends," Michael said.

"You have new friends? Who are they?" Nick asked.

Michael stood up to give his old friends a hug. It had been quite a while since their last visit. "One day when I was cleaning I found this room. It was locked, but I managed to break it open. When I was inside I found this."

Lily interrupted, and said, "What is it called?"

"This is called a Makulip. Growing up, I had heard stories about the Makulip, but I never saw one. I remember one day when I was only ten years old, I heard one of the older Taemites talking about this transportation device. He said that when we were in danger, the Taemites would simply wave the Makulip, then magically be transported back home to where the Taemites actually originated from."

Hardly able to believe their ears, Lily asked, "Can we go there with you?"

Nick looked at Lily, trying not to let on how dangerous he believed this idea actually was.

"I don't think that would be safe. Remember, they are Taemites and they don't like humans." Michael said, trying to protect his friends from being harmed.

"We promise to stay directly behind you, and I still I have my necklace made from Lazenfront. If we're careful, they won't see us," Lily continued, pleading.

Finally, after being convinced, Michael agreed.

This new mystery was going to be the most exciting point in all of their summer vacation.

Michael took the Makulip in his hand, and said, "Hold hands and don't let go. This is going to make you feel really dizzy," as he pointed the Makulip directly at their reflection in the mirror, causing a loud explosion. BOOM!

Lily and Nick grew extremely dizzy and were about to fall down when suddenly... BOOM!!! Lily and Nick had arrived at the land called Strapron.

"Wow, it's beautiful here!" exclaimed Lily.

"I've never seen a place with so much color. Look at the trees," Nick said.

The trees weren't green; instead they were rainbow colored.

"Michael, how many times have you been here?" Lily asked.

"I have been here every day. I feel like this is my home. I'm not lonely here. The best part is, I met a new friend here. His name is Paglen," Michael said, trying to convince his friends of how happy he was here.

"Can we go exploring?" Lily asked.

"We have to be careful, there are some Taemites that would kill you if they knew you were here," Michael said, trying to warn his friends.

"Is Paglen dangerous to us?" Nick asked, trying not to sound scared.

"Paglen has never met a human before. I told him about both of you and he said he wanted to meet real humans. So, if you promise to be careful, I'll take you to where he lives," Michael added.

"Of course we will!" exclaimed Lily.

The adventure was going to take an even more enticing twist.

As the three friends continued on with their walk, suddenly the ground began shaking.

"What's that?" Nick asked.

"Hurry, we have to hide!" Michael screamed.

Nick, Lily and Michael jumped behind a big bush. Right then a huge ostrich-looking creature came running past them.

"What was that?" Lily asked Michael.

"That was the Ostmin. They are here to protect the Taemites from unwanted visitors. Usually they stay at the edge by the lake. I don't know why he was this close to the village," Michael said, trying to figure out if this was such a good idea after all. "*I* think we need to get you both out of here," Michael continued.

"Can we meet Paglen before we leave? He's never met a human before. I promise after that we can leave," Lily begged.

"Alright, but we've got to be extremely careful!" Michael said.

Finally after what seemed like hours they arrived at Paglen's house.

The house looked like a giant mushroom. Michael stomped his foot on the ground and suddenly the door opened. "Let's go," Michael said.

They slowly walked inside, not sure as to what they were about to see.

Suddenly, right before their eyes was this strange looking creature. He was covered in yellow fur. Lily and Nick stood frozen not knowing what to do or say.

"This is Paglen," Michael said.

Lily held her hand out and gradually Paglen touched it. "Wow, he's so soft." Lily said.

Nick was not as confident in being able to actually touch this stranger.

"Come on, Nick, it's okay," Lily said.

Nick decided it would be all right and reached his hand out to touch Paglen. "You're right, he is soft!" Nick exclaimed.

Michael introduced his friends.

Lily had so many questions for Paglen, but she tried to remain calm. "Have you ever been to Michael's place?" Lily asked.

"I have never left Strapron. I've been too scared of humans," Paglen said.

They were actually enjoying spending time getting to know Paglen, when a loud siren began sounding.

"What is that!" Nick shouted.

Paglen stood up, and shouted, "Hurry you must hide!"

Nick and Lily were scared and didn't know what was happening.

Michael yelled at them, "Follow me!"

Paglen took his friends to a secret location.

"What is this place?" Nick asked.

"This is where I go when I need to disappear for a while," Paglen said.

Standing up, Lily began looking around the room.

"Michael, this looks like the room at your place," Nick said as he began looking around and found a book in the corner. "What is this book?" Nick asked.

Paglen came to retrieve the book from Nick. "This is the only thing that I have left of my family," Paglen said.

"Can we look at it? Lily asked.

"Yes, I suppose that would be fine," Paglen said, handing his most prized possession to his visitors.

Inside the book were pictures of Paglen's family.

"What happened to your family?" Nick asked.

"One day creatures wanting to kill us invaded our village. They gathered everyone they could find and put them in this big pit and burned them all," Paglen said, feeling sad about this loss.

"Eventually the creatures left and slowly the survivors came out from their hiding places. The remaining Taemites decided that from that day forward they would not allow any other visitors into our land," Michael continued for his friend.

"What was that siren for?" Lily asked.

"That's a warning that trespassers have been spotted in our village," Paglen said.

Michael stood up, and said, "We need to leave here now!"

The danger was now evident, and it was extremely necessary to get Nick and Lily back home.

Michael and Paglen decided to leave Lily and Nick hiding in the secret room while they explored a route that could be used to escape.

Meanwhile, back in the secret room, Lily was becoming increasingly anxious and wanted to do some exploring. "Nick, I'll be right back. I'm going to look around outside," Lily said.

"No! You have to stay here. It's too dangerous outside!" Nick said, trying to convince Lily to stay in the room.

Of course Lily was very stubborn and went exploring anyway.

Lily very carefully opened the door, and even more carefully slipped outside. While outside, she heard a funny sound coming from behind Paglen's house. Lily was now in detective mode, so she continued very carefully to where the sound was coming from.

As Lily got closer, the sound became more familiar. She

couldn't believe her eyes. Right before her stood a man. Lily thought to herself, *That can't be right. Humans don't live here. Why is that man here?*

Lily decided to return back to the secret room and fill Nick in on what she had just discovered.

"Nick, guess what I saw?" Lily asked trying to contain her excitement.

"How can I guess?" Nick replied.

"I saw a man right behind this house. He was a human," Lily said.

"What is he doing here?" Nick asked.

This new case was once again beginning to take a new twist. Just as Lily was getting excited about trying to figure out who the man was, Paglen and Michael returned.

"Let's go. We found a way to sneak out without being seen," Michael ordered his friends.

"No, we can't leave yet. I saw a man standing right outside back behind Paglen's house," Lily reported.

"I thought I told you to stay in here!" Michael yelled.

"I tried to tell her, but she wouldn't listen to me," Nick said.

"Listen Michael, I saw a man. Paglen, do you know who he was?" Lily asked.

"No. There aren't any other humans in our village," Paglen said.

"What about that siren? Remember, that meant there was a sighting of a trespasser. I bet it was him," Nick said, beginning to become excited.

"Fine. If we stay you must do what Paglen and I say. Do you agree with that?" Michael asked.

"Yes!" Lily and Nick said in unison.

Paglen led his new friends to a location where they would be able to investigate who this man actually was.

The path they walked was full of strange looking creatures. "What are those?" Lily asked.

"Those are little Wizzles; they are usually used for sending messages to someone," Paglen replied.

"Are they nice?" Nick asked.

"Yes," Michael said, as he reached to grab one. Michael took the Wizzle and handed it to Nick.

"Oh, they are nice," Nick said as he nuzzled his face into the soft feathers of this strange little creature. "Can I have one? I promise I won't let anyone see it," Nick asked.

"No, they wouldn't survive outside of this village," Paglen said.

Feeling a little disappointed, Nick and Lily put these little creatures back down on the ground and continued on with their journey.

As they neared their destination, Lily once again heard that familiar sound. "Listen! Do you hear that?" Lily asked.

"Yes, I think it's coming from down there by that large rock," Nick said.

"That's not a rock. That's what we use to renew our food source," Paglen said.

"How does it work?" Lily asked.

"We go and put a cooking cup on top, then after a few seconds our cup is full of food," Paglen said.

They very slowly approached this mysterious man.

The closer they came, the more worried Michael was becoming. "He looks so familiar to me," Michael said.

At that very moment, Nick let out a loud sneeze.

The stranger had now seen them. Michael and Paglen stood in front of Lily and Nick. Lily and Nick knew that their very lives were in extreme danger. The stranger slowly moved closer to them.

Michael once again looked closer at the stranger and asked, "What is your name?"

The man stood motionless, not muttering a sound. "What is your name?" Michael asked again.

Nothing. The stranger just stood there.

"Maybe he can't talk?" Lily asked.

Paglen looked at the man, then closed his eyes. Suddenly the man began moving very slightly.

"What is Paglen doing?" Nick asked.

"He is communicating with him through telepathy," Michael answered.

After a while, Paglen told them the man's name was Jesper. He had come here in search of his family.

"Why does he look human?" Lily asked Paglen.

Paglen closed his eyes to communicate this question to Jesper. "He only takes on this form to hide his real identity," Paglen said.

"Why was he making that loud sound?" Nick asked.

"He was calling out for his family," Paglen added.

"I guess then we can continue on with getting Nick and Lily out of this place," Michael said.

As they turned to tell Jesper goodbye, he was gone. He completely disappeared.

"Where did he go?" Lily asked.

"I don't know, but we've got to get out of here!" Michael ordered.

It was time to resume the walk toward their upcoming escape.

As they continued on with their walk, suddenly Michael yelled, "I remember who that man is now! I saw a picture of him when I was a young child. I was warned about how dangerous he was to us. This man was brought to kill all Taemites," Michael said.

"Do you think that he's the creature that killed Paglen's family?" Lily asked.

"That's exactly who killed my family," Paglen said.

Lily and Nick were not about to leave Strapron now. They wanted to make sure their new friend was going to be safe. These friends needed to ensure the safety for all of the inhabitants of this village and the continued existence of all Taemites, even though their very lives would be in extreme danger. The group of friends headed back toward Paglen's house to come up with a plan on how to banish the evil creature back to the land of the unknown. Nick and Lily knew that this case was definitely going to be the most dangerous of all.

The decision of how to stop this creature was one that needed to be made with the most cautious planning. The brainstorming soon began.

"How about we trick the man into a trap. Kinda like capturing a rabbit in a box," Nick said, hoping that his plan would work.

"No I don't think that would work. This creature is very intelligent and would never fall into such a basic trap," Paglen said.

"How about using me as a part of the trap? I would go out looking for him. Once I found him, I would tell him that I wanted to help him find his family. He doesn't know that we know who he actually is," Lily said.

"No! I won't let you do anything that dangerous. Let's keep thinking," Michael said.

Hours went by and no other ideas came close to being able to capture this creature.

"My plan will work. Please, Michael, let me do this for Paglen and for you. I promise, I'm a tough girl. I can do this and, besides, you guys are going to be close by so if anything does happen you can come and rescue me," Lily said, hoping that her idea would be accepted.

"Michael, it will be okay. We won't let anything happen to Lily," Paglen said softly to his friend.

Lily's plan was accepted, even though Nick was afraid that something might happen to his partner in crime. He agreed to help implement Lily's strategy.

Now that the plan was set, all that needed to be done was to actually begin. Lily would lead the man into Paglen's room, then Paglen would banish him into a steel container using the Makulip.

Lily walked out onto the same path that they had last seen the man. Hopefully, he would be somewhere fairly close. Lily kept walking, her heart beating faster with anticipation of what was to come. She was paying close attention to her surroundings because her experience as a detective told her that the enemy could turn up when you least expect it. All was extremely quiet, not a single sound could be heard. Although Lily knew her friends were close by, she was still pretty scared.

Just as Lily was about to turn around and surrender to the possibility of failing to catch this creature, she heard the familiar sound. Lily slowly walked toward the noise. Each step was drawing Lily closer to the unknown. Finally she was directly behind the man. "Excuse me. I was wondering if you found your family yet?" Lily asked.

Once again the man stood silent. Remembering how Paglen communicated with him, she closed her eyes and concentrated harder than she ever had. Nothing happened. "Okay, Lily, you can do this. Just believe," Lily said, trying to convince herself that this would work. She closed her eyes, then heard a voice in her head. It was working. Lily tried to remain calm. She telepathically repeated her question. *"Have you found your family yet?"*

The voice answered, *"No. I can't find them."*

Once again Lily closed her eyes and asked, *"Do you want me to help?"*

The voice said, *"That would be great."*

The plan was working. Lily and the creature began searching for the missing family members.

As the day progressed, Lily was trying to figure out how to get this man to Paglen's room.

While Lily was working on befriending this creature, Michael, Nick and Paglen remained close by.

Nick was getting more worried as each minute passed. "I think we need to get closer. Lily and the man are too far ahead of us," Nick pleaded.

"Nick, don't worry. Lily's a smart girl. I won't let anything happen to her. Remember, she's our friend too," Michael said trying to calm Nick down.

Suddenly they heard a loud scream.

"What was that? That wasn't Lily was it?" Nick asked, trying not to let his fear make more out of it than necessary.

"I don't know. Let's go look for Lily," Michael replied.

Slowly, Nick, Paglen and Michael made their way toward the direction of the scream. Looking in every direction, Lily could not be seen.

"Where did she go?" Paglen asked.

The three split up in order to cover more territory.

All of a sudden Nick screamed for Paglen and Michael, "Hey over here!"

As Michael and Paglen made their way toward Nick, they noticed that Nick had Lily's backpack in his hands.

"This is Lily's. Something's happened to her. She never goes anywhere without this," Nick said, growing more concerned with each thought of the danger that Lily was now facing. "What are we going to do now?" Nick asked.

"I think it's time to go and ask for help from the other Taemites," Paglen said.

"We can't, they don't like humans," Michael said.

"That's our only chance of rescuing Lily," Paglen replied.

"If you say they won't hurt my friends, then let's go," Michael said, hoping that the Taemites would be able to help his friend Lily.

Paglen led the way to the Taemites. Nick walked behind Michael just in case they wanted to harm him.

Once inside, Paglen went to the leader and filled him in on what was happening.

The leader of the Taemites was extremely appreciative of Lily and Nick for trying to banish this creature. Because of this, they were ready to rescue Lily from this dangerous being. The leader ordered all of the men Taemites out to search the village for Lily and the creature. "No matter what happens, do not kill the creature. I want anyone who finds them to bring both of them directly to me. Is that understood?" the leader asked.

The army of Taemites went immediately into the woods. While the search was underway, Nick grew increasingly more impatient. "I've got to do something. I can't just sit around and do nothing," Nick said.

"No, we have to stay here, just in case Lily manages to trick the man into Paglen's room," Michael said, trying to convince Nick that the plan still might actually work.

The day faded into night and still no word from Lily.

Lily woke up and knew she was in trouble. The creature had somehow managed to trap her in some sort of cave. Lily began screaming, hoping that her friends would hear her. Lily searched for her backpack. She always kept all types of tools in it. There had to be something in it that she could use to escape from this prison. Lily searched frantically for her backpack, but she couldn't find it.

Suddenly the man returned.

"Why did you put me in here?" Lily asked, still trying to act like his friend.

"I don't have any missing family. I know you figured out who I am and I can't let you go," the creature said.

"You talked. I thought you couldn't speak," Lily asked.

"That was my way of getting you into my trap. You see, it worked!" the creature said.

"So what do you really look like? You said that you were using a disguise," Lily asked.

The creature raised his arms above his head, then the next second he was a two-headed dragon.

Lily was more scared now than she had ever been in her entire life. She backed up in her cage, not sure as to what this creature wanted to do to her.

"I need to leave for a while. You be good and stay here." The creature left Lily in her cage.

Trapped like an animal, Lily dropped to the floor and softly started to cry. Lily had never felt the need to cry, but this time was different. Lily just sat on the floor of her prison and cried softly for someone to come rescue her.

The army of Taemites was getting closer to the cave that was now Lily's home. A group found the cave and went inside in order to search for this missing girl.

Lily heard the commotion and stood up. Standing in her cage, trapped and scared, Lily screamed.

"Don't be scared. We are here to help you," one Taemite told her.

Lily now knew that they were there to rescue her. Just as they were about to break open the cage, the evil dragon returned. It made the loudest shrill sound that actually made parts of the cave begin to crumble.

The army of Taemites started shooting the dragon with devices used to paralyze the creature. The dragon struggled and fought with a great deal of strength before finally giving into the inevitable. The dragon dropped to the floor. He couldn't move. Lily was safe.

She walked up to the dragon and said, "I guess you're trapped now!"

The Taemites took Lily and the dragon back to the leader as they were previously ordered.

Where are you taking me?" Lily asked.

"We have to bring both of you back to the leader. He will know what to do next."

Lily had a funny feeling that she still was in danger, but, nonetheless, went with them.

Lily was now face to face with the leader of the Taemites.

The leader looked at Lily and asked, "Are you alright?"

Trying to act brave, Lily replied, "I'm fine. Can I return to my friends?" The danger was hopefully over, or so Lily hoped.

"Yes you are free to leave. You and your friends need to leave Strapron immediately before something else happens to you."

"I am definitely leaving right now!" Lily added enthusiastically. As Lily was leaving, the detective mode returned. Something deep inside her knew that something was just not right. She quietly snuck closer to hear what the leader was saying to the army.

She couldn't believe her ears, the leader said to bring the dragon to him. Lily stayed still, anticipating the answer behind the mystery of this creature. Finally the leader was standing beside the dragon and all of a sudden, the dragon returned to his man disguise. The leader and the man sat down.

Lily couldn't believe it! They were acting as if they were friends. "I don't know why you sent your army after me. I had her. She is the answer to our problem," the man said.

"You must trust me. I know you are anxious to take power of Strapron, but you must be patient. Do you understand?" the leader replied.

"Fine, but it better be soon," the man said.

"Right now I want you to return to where I told you to go, and this time stay there until I send for you!" the leader ordered.

The man disappeared into a cloud of smoke.

Lily now knew that the mystery of this creature was far from being solved.

Lily quickly returned to Paglen's house. She rushed inside, and her friends were very excited to see her safe and sound.

"Oh, Lily, I was so worried about you!" Nick exclaimed.

"I'm fine. I know more about the creature. He and the leader are working together to take control over all of the Taemites," Lily said, trying not to talk to fast, as she often did when she was excited.

"What are you talking about?" Michael asked.

"The leader is our friend. He makes sure that we all are safe. Why would you think he was trying to harm any of us?" Paglen asked.

"I'm telling you the truth. Your leader is not what he is letting everyone to believe. The creature left, but I don't know where he went," Lily said.

"Well, there's not much more we can do right now. I want all of us to leave and get you both to your home," Michael said.

"I can't leave now. Paglen won't be safe!" Lily added.

"Maybe Paglen could come back with us?" Nick asked.

"No. This is my home. I won't leave it. Don't worry, I'll be fine," Paglen said.

"I'll come back and visit to make sure you are fine," Michael said, hoping to convince Lily that everything was going to be fine.

The decision was made. It was time for Nick and Lily to return home.

Lily ran up to Paglen and gave him a big hug. "I'm going to miss you!" Lily cried.

"Don't worry, we'll see each other again," Paglen said.

Nick, Lily and Michael left their friend behind, hoping that he would be all right. They grabbed hands once again, and Michael pointed the Makulip at them. Suddenly they were transported back to Michael's tree.

Lily and Nick were safe from harm now that they were back in Michael's room.

"Please keep an eye on Paglen. I don't think we've seen the last of that creature," Lily said.

The three friends hugged and the duo left Michael's tree.

"What time is it? We must have been gone a really long time," Nick asked.

"What? That can't be right." Lily said as she looked at her watch. "It says it's only 1:00 p.m."

Somehow time had stood still during their adventure into the land of Strapron. These detectives had discovered another magical mystery that involved the Taemites.

"Nothing surprises me any more when it comes to the Taemites," Lily said.

Lily and Nick quickly got on their bikes to return home. It had been an extremely busy day and both of the sleuths were tired.

Lily was so exhausted she didn't eat much dinner later that evening. Her family knew that when Lily was that tired she must have had an exciting day. Lily slept all night without any of her usual dreams.

The next couple of days went by fast, and Lily soon found herself getting dressed for her first day of school.

This was going to be Lily and Nick's last year in middle school; something that she should have been excited about, but Lily was still distracted about the man she had seen in Strapron. Feeling like the excitement of the summer was a thing of the past, Lily was dreading the fact that her adventures were finished with until next summer.

As usual Nick rode his bike over to Lily's house so they could ride together. "Hi, Lily. Are you ready for school?" Nick asked.

"I don't think it matters. Come on, let's go. Maybe something exciting will happen at school," Lily said.

The ride over was the same as it always was.

The school was full of activity. Everyone was busy talking about his or her summers. Lily and Nick knew that even though they would love to tell everyone about all of their adventures this summer; they knew that was going to have to remain a secret between the two of them. Lily and Nick had to go to their different classrooms, but agreed to meet up at the cafeteria.

Lily looked at her schedule. She noticed that the teacher in her first class was new to their school. Lily thought about how exciting that might be. She walked in and found a desk and sat down. The room was full of students chattering away, waiting for the teacher to arrive to start class.

Lily got out her book and began flipping through it. As she did the teacher walked in. He was carrying a load of books in his arms, so Lily couldn't see his face. Finally he dropped the books onto his desk and turned around. Lily let out a loud gasp. She couldn't believe her eyes. It couldn't be, or could it? Lily's new teacher was the man that she and Nick had seen when they were in Strapron. Lily tried to remain calm and pretend that she didn't recognize him.

The new teacher introduced himself. "My name is Mr. Wilkens. I want all of you to call me Jesper. After all, I hope we can all be friends."

Lily slowly slipped down in her chair and tried desperately to be invisible. Unfortunately for Lily, Mr. Wilkens noticed her.

"Hi. Do I know you?" asked Mr. Wilkens.

"No, I don't think so," Lily responded.

"If you say so."

Classes that day went by so slowly, that it seemed like weeks before it was finally time for lunch.

At last lunchtime had finally arrived and now Lily could tell Nick about her latest discovery.

Lily sat down at the table and opened up her lunch box. Trying to eat, Lily waited impatiently for Nick. As she was about to give up on seeing Nick for lunch, he finally came walking up to the table.

"Nick, you're not going to believe who my new teacher is!" Lily reported.

"I don't have a clue!" Nick said.

"He's the man from Strapron. I think he recognized me though," Lily worriedly said.

"Why would he come here to Scott City?" Nick asked.

"I'm pretty sure it has to do with what he started in Strapron," Lily said.

"What are we going to do?" Nick asked, even though he already knew what the answer was going to be.

"You know exactly what we're going to do!" Lily replied.

This school year was not going to be as boring as what Lily had originally thought. Who knows, maybe there was more detective work that needed to be done in order to save the Taemites...

Chapter Six
The New Teacher

The school year in Scott City was usually nothing special, but this year seemed to be very promising for the duo. Lily and Nick both agreed that this new teacher was definitely worth some investigating. There was one small problem that the two sleuths faced in solving the mystery of this new teacher; how would they be able to investigate while they were required to attend classes.

"I don't know how we can solve this case while we're in school," Nick said, sounding defeated.

"Nick, private detectives never think like that. There's always a way!" Lily exclaimed.

"Lunch is almost over. We'd better get to our next classes," Nick reminded.

"Okay, but let's meet at my house on Saturday morning. Hopefully, by then we'll have an idea on how to investigate Mr. Wilkens," Lily said.

Lily went on to her next class, but she simply could not get the image of Mr. Wilkens as the man from Strapron out of her head.

Each morning Lily tried to discover something about Mr. Wilkens. Finally, on Friday, she got her first big break.

During class, Mr. Wilkens made an announcement. "Since this is my first year at Scott City Middle School, I thought it might be fun to go on a field trip. I want to know how many of you would enjoy going camping up in the woods in Denver, Colorado?" Mr. Wilkens asked, already knowing the answer.

The entire class cheered an extremely loud, "YEAH!"

All except Lily, who secretly knew that this new teacher was up to something.

Trying to regain control of his students, Mr. Wilkens said, "Okay, class, I'm happy you are all excited, but you need to calm down so we can discuss the arrangements."

Everyone sat back down in their seats and was eager to make the plans.

"This field trip is going to be a little expensive, so, with that said, I need some ideas for a fund raiser?" Mr. Wilkens asked.

Suddenly the room was filled with students raising their hands with ideas that might make this field trip a reality.

"Wow, that's a lot of suggestions. How about you, Lily. Do you have any ideas?" Mr. Wilkens asked.

"Um, no, I don't think so," Lily quickly replied.

"Well, you think about it for a while and let me know if you think of one, okay?" Mr. Wilkens asked.

Lily simply nodded.

Each of the ideas were pretty basic. Some included a yard sale, a cookie sale, and even a raffle drive, but Mr. Wilkens didn't think they would bring in enough money that was needed to help with the expense of the field trip.

"Let's take a few days and maybe someone will get a really good idea," Mr. Wilkens said.

All Lily could think of during this commotion was that Mr. Wilkens was not really a teacher. He wasn't even a human. Lily was going to prove this, not only to herself, but also to the other students.

Saturday arrived, and now it was time to get started on this new case. Lily woke up early Saturday and ran downstairs.

"Wow, why are you up so early?" Lily's mom asked.

"Nick's going to come over. We have some investigating to do," Lily said.

"I guess you must have found a new case. Where did you find this one?" Mom asked.

"Well, I can't really say. It's a secret," Lily said, hoping her mom would not ask any further questions.

"Oh, I see. I'll leave you to your secret duties." Mom said, as she smiled and continued on with her weekend responsibilities.

Lily went outside to wait for Nick to arrive. While she was waiting, she couldn't believe her eyes. The neighbor across the street, Mrs. Smith, had a visitor at her house. Mrs. Smith rarely had any visitors since her husband had died a few years ago, and her children very seldom visited. Lily always felt sorry for her. Mrs. Smith's door opened, and right before her eyes Lily noticed that Mr. Wilkens was the visitor.

Trying not to let her new teacher see her, Lily dashed quickly inside. Lily peeked through the blinds and waited for Mr. Wilkens to drive away.

Lily returned to the porch to wait for her partner. Nick rode up on his bicycle and noticed that Lily seemed unusually excited.

"What's wrong, Lily?" Nick asked.

"You aren't going to believe this!" Lily exclaimed.

"What?" Nick asked, getting more excited by the second.

"Mrs. Smith had a visitor this morning," Lily said casually.

"So what if she had a visitor," Nick said, sounding frustrated in trying to get information from Lily.

"The visitor was Mr. Wilkens," Lily said, with a big smile on her face.

"How does your new teacher know Mrs. Smith?" Nick asked.

"That's a good question! I think we need to go over and visit with Mrs. Smith. Maybe she will help us learn more about Mr. Wilkens," Lily said.

"I don't understand how your neighbor would know this man, especially if he really is the creature from Strapron," Nick said.

"I don't know, but I do know that he looks like the same man we saw in Strapron," Lily replied.

The duo left to begin the investigation for this new mystery.

Lily grabbed some flowers from her mom's rose bushes to give to Mrs. Smith. This would get them into the house. She rang the doorbell, and within seconds Mrs. Smith was at the door. Mrs. Smith was a short, round looking woman in her seventies.

"Hi, Mrs. Smith. I brought you some flowers," Lily said, trying to sound loveable.

"Oh, how sweet of you, darling. Won't you both come inside?" Mrs. Smith said.

The detectives were now ready to begin this investigation.

"Mrs. Smith, this is my friend Nick," Lily said.

"Nice to meet you, Nick. Would you like some blueberry muffins? I just took them out of the oven," Mrs. Smith asked.

"Sure!" Nick said, never turning down any offer of free food.

Mrs. Smith returned shortly carrying a tray with muffins and two glasses of milk.

"Yum, these taste really good!" Nick exclaimed.

Lily nodded with agreement. "I was sitting on my porch this morning and I noticed you had a visitor," Lily said.

"Yes, that was Jesper Wilkens. He is my grandson, just moved here from San Francisco, California. Jesper is teaching at the middle school here in town. Aren't you both in middle school? Maybe you have seen him around school?" Mrs. Smith asked.

"Yes, he is my new teacher for science," Lily replied. Even though Lily had her suspicions about Jesper Wilkens, she was not going to let anyone else other than Nick in on her belief.

"How long did Mr. Wilkens live in California?" Nick asked.

"He has lived there his whole life," Mrs. Smith said.

"Which one of your children are his parents?" Lily asked.

"Jesper was adopted when he was ten years old by my eldest daughter and her husband," Mrs. Smith added.

"Well, we'd better get going. We are going to go visit some friends. Thanks for the milk and muffins," Lily said.

The two detectives left, now with a plan on how to uncover the true identity of Mr. Wilkens.

"Well, Lily, do you still believe that your new teacher is the same man we saw in Strapron?" Nick asked.

"I think that we need to learn more about this adoption, so we need to go to the library," Lily said.

Lily and Nick jumped on their bikes and headed towards the library.

While riding to the library, Lily's head was full of different schemes in which they could reveal the true identity of Mr. Wilkens. The hard part was figuring out which would be the best.

Once inside the library, Lily went and asked Ms. Carroll where to find information about adoptions.

"I think there is a website on the computer that can be more help than I can. What are you two up to now?" Ms. Carroll asked.

"We have a paper we have to write about adoptions for school." Lily said, sounding even believable to Nick.

"Oh, alright then. Let me know if you need some more help," Ms. Carroll said.

Lily sat down at the computer and began searching for the website Ms. Carroll had mentioned earlier. "I can't find it!" Lily exclaimed.

"Let me see," Nick said as Lily got up to let Nick work his impressive computer skills.

"See, you can't find it either," Lily said.

"Wait. Just wait. There it is, right there." Nick said, with a huge grin on his face.

Lily sat back down in front of the computer and searched for records involving the adoption of Mr. Wilkens. Finally, within minutes, the information they desperately wanted was right before their eyes.

"Let's see. It says that on June 17, 1981, a child was adopted to Mr. and Mrs. Roger Wilkens." The child's name was not given, but this had to be the adoption for which they were searching. "There's not anything in this that's going to help," Lily said, feeling more frustrated than before in any of the other cases.

"We do know that Mr. Wilkens appears to be around in his thirties, just like the child in this record would be," Nick stated, reviving Lily's interest in this new case.

"Let's get back over to my house and figure out a way to learn more about Mr. Wilkens," Lily said.

Lily and Nick went straight into Lily's bedroom and got started on the brainstorming what needed to be done in order to solve this unusual case. Ideas were rushing to both of the detectives, but nothing really seemed like the perfect plot. Just as the two were about to take a break and have some lunch, Lily had a brilliant idea.

"Nick, I've got it! In class Mr. Wilkens told the class we were going to go on a field trip to Colorado," Lily said.

"Wow that sounds fun!" Nick shouted.

"That's not the point. We have to have a fundraiser to come up with some money to help pay for the expense of this field trip. So, I think if we spend some personal time with him alone, then maybe we can learn more about his true identity," Lily said with a big smile on her face.

"Okay, but how are we going to do that?" Nick asked.

"Well, if we have a school carnival we'll have no choice but to spend extra time with him," Lily said.

"You're right, that just might work. Lily, what if you're right and your new teacher is the creature from Strapron? It's going to get really dangerous," Nick stated, trying to make sure that the two of them would not come into any harm.

"Let's go and see if we can talk Michael into coming out of seclusion to help us. I think he will, if he believes his friend is going to be in danger," Lily said, hoping this was going to be the situation.

Lily and Nick jumped back on their bikes in order to fill Michael in on the new plan. The two detectives rode faster on their bikes than they ever had before. Soon the duo was inside Michael's house.

"Hi, Michael. We have a problem and we want you to help us." Nick said.

"What's the problem first?" Michael said, already knowing that these two were usually up to something that more times than not were going to turn out being dangerous.

"I have a new teacher in school. You're not going to believe this!" Lily exclaimed.

"Just try me." Michael said.

"His name is Jesper Wilkens." Lily continued.

"Why does that name sound so familiar to me?" Michael asked.

"That's because he might be the creature that we saw when we were in Strapron." Nick said.

"Remember, the man said his name was Jesper when Paglan spoke with him. Anyway, we have to uncover the truth behind him in order to rescue Paglan from danger." Lily said.

"How do you both plan on doing that?" Michael asked.

"We are going to have a school carnival and we will have to spend extra time with him outside of school," Nick said.

"That's not all, though. We need your help. If he is the same creature, it's going to be too dangerous for us alone, and we need your help," Lily said, hoping this would work to convince Michael to come out of hiding.

"I can't come outside. If anybody sees me, it will frighten them senseless," Michael said.

"Nobody is going to be scared if we clean you up. Remember, you are human too. All you need is some good cleaning," Lily said.

Michael was convinced this actually might work, so the three set in for some major cleaning of Michael.

The cleaning process involved having Michael bathe down in the creek. While Michael was bathing, Lily took off her backpack and got out all of her supplies, which contsisted of scissors, a razor and shaving cream.

Michael returned from his bath, and although he still did not quite look human, at least he did look cleaner. "What are you going with those? Is that going to hurt?" Michael asked as he saw the scissors.

"No, I promise. I'm going to cut your hair, then I'm going to shave your face," Lily said.

"Have you ever done this before?" Michael asked.

"Well, no, but I don't think it is that hard. If it hurts, than I'll let Nick take over," Lily said tenderly.

The transformation was now started, and before long all of the long dark hair was gone and now Michael's face was revealed.

"Okay, that's done. Let's start the shaving process," Lily said.

"You know what, Lily, I've watched my dad shave a lot of times. Let me try this, okay?" Nick recommended.

Making sure not to hurt or scare him, Nick very gently removed all of the long facial hair from Michael. Finally came the time for him to look in the mirror to see the new Michael.

"I look like a human. I can't believe this. This is actually going to work," Michael said eagerly.

"I can't believe you didn't have faith in us," Lily said teasingly.

"Well, Michael, it's getting late. We'll come back tomorrow to get everything prepared for your return to society," Lily told Michael.

The three friends exchanged goodbyes and parted ways. Lily and Nick headed home. Now was not the time to get into trouble for being outside too late.

Later that evening, Lily was having dinner with her mom and dad.

"I have a new teacher this year. His name is Mr. Wilkens. He is Mrs. Smith's grandson. He is going to take us on a field trip to Colorado. Mr. Wilkens asked for suggestions for fundraisers and I thought having a school carnival would bring in a lot of money. What do you both think about that?" Lily asked, trying not to talk too quickly, as she often did when she was excited.

"I think that's a really good idea," Dad replied.

Mom agreed as well. "Let us know if you need some help," Mom added.

"I will, but I probably will be spending extra time at school to help out with the plans," Lily said, hoping this would be believable to her parents.

"Sure, that's fine," Dad said.

Lily's plan was once again coming together as it always seemed to do.

Lily rushed through dinner and headed for bed. As always Lily was eager to get some sleep, just so she could get some clues to solving each mystery. This case was no different from the others, and once again Lily depended on getting answers through her dreams.

At first, sleep didn't come as quickly as it usually did. Lily tossed around in bed, getting more frustrated as the time passed by. Suddenly without any hint of coming, sleep had finally arrived.

This dream seemed a little more unusual than any of the others. This time Lily was inside a house that was completely unfamiliar. Lily began walking around to see if she could see anyone. Suddenly, she heard voices coming from a room. Lily quietly walked to where the voices were coming from and listened. She listened intently for some clue as to whom these voices belonged. The conversation was about a takeover of some secret project.

Lily tried to get closer so she could possibly identify whom the people were, but as she did, she accidentally knocked a lamp off a small table that she was standing beside. Lily quickly dashed into a small closet to hide from being discovered. The door of the closet had blinds across the front; this enabled Lily to watch as the people came out of the room to investigate the loud crash they heard. The moment had come to see these unidentified individuals.

Lily couldn't believe her eyes. The voices belonged to Mrs. Smith and Mr. Wilkens. Lily grew even more interested in explaining why they would be talking about some special project. Lily was so focused on trying to understand what the conversation was about, that she had not realized that standing right beside her was a white cat. Normally this would not have been a problem for most people, except that for Lily this presented a dilemma, because she was allergic to cats.

Before she had a chance to stop it from happening, the unthinkable happened. Lily let out a very loud sneeze. Her cover was now blown, and Lily was only seconds from being discovered.

Suddenly Lily's alarm clock went off, waking her up at the most opportune moment. Sitting up in bed, Lily's heart was beating very fast. It was even a little difficult for her to catch her breath. This dream was going to be a little harder to understand, but even so, Lily was eager to get over to Nick's house to fill him in on this bizarre dream.

The morning already held a lot of events for the two sleuths, and now even more was to be presented.

Lily arrived at Nick's house very early, but, much to her surprise, Nick was already waiting for her on his porch.

"Nick, I had a dream last night," Lily said.

"So, was there anything that will help us with this case?" Nick asked.

"I don't know. My dream was strange. I was in a house and I heard voices coming from a room, so I listened, but I didn't recognize them. Then I accidentally knocked a lamp off a table and I had to hide inside a closet. I thought I was safe, when all of a sudden I let out a sneeze. Just as I was about to be discovered, my alarm clock went off and woke me up," Lily said.

"So you couldn't see their faces?" Nick asked.

"I didn't say that," Lily snapped.

"Well then, who were they?" Nick asked again.

"They were Mrs. Smith and Mr. Wilkens. They were talking about some takeover of a secret project," Lily continued.

"What do you think that means?" Nick questioned.

"I'm not sure, but I bet it has to do with Strapron," Lily said. "Let's get over to Michael's and tell him. Maybe he has some ideas about this dream," Lily added.

The two detectives headed back into the woods to hopefully uncover some of these mysteries that seemed to surround Mr. Wilkens.

The duo arrived shortly at Michael's house and told him about this odd dream.

"What do you think the secret project is?" Nick asked.

"I can only guess it has something to do with the termination of all Taemites. If you are right, Lily, then this pretty much tells us that your new teacher is the creature we met in Strapron," Michael said.

"My dreams always help us. I just can't figure out why sweet Mrs. Smith would be involved with something as evil as this seems to be," Lily said.

"There's something that we are missing. Mrs. Smith just can't be involved with the destruction of Strapron," Nick stated. "I think we need to figure out how to get Michael involved with the investigation of your new teacher."

Lily always had a plan, and this time was not any different. "I am going to introduce Michael as my uncle who is visiting from California. When I go to school tomorrow, I will tell Mr. Wilkens about having a school carnival as a fundraiser. Mr. Wilkens will agree to this suggestion, at which time I will tell him about my Uncle Michael visiting from California, and how he would really like to help," Lily said, smiling, feeling proud that she had already come up with a plan without any help.

"What if your teacher doesn't like the idea of having a school carnival?" Nick asked.

"Don't worry, he will," Lily said without any doubt. "Now, for you Michael, we have to come up with a made up past that you can casually reveal about yourself," Lily said.

"How about Michael says that when he lived in San Francisco, he worked at a zoo," Nick suggested.

"I don't know anything about zoos," Michael replied.

"It's okay, we'll make something up that you can say. Let's see, how about you worked at the zoo in San Francisco for ten years. You decided to take some time off work to write a book and decided coming to Scott City would be a nice quiet place to complete the book," Lily said.

"I don't know how you come with these ideas," Michael stated.

"Anyway, I brought some of my dad's clothes for you to wear. I think they should fit," Lily said, as she opened up her backpack to retrieve the clothing.

"Do you think anybody will be suspicious of me?" Michael asked.

"Why would they? When you are dressed in normal clothes, you look any typical person," Nick said.

"I think you two need to get going. I've got a lot of things to do before I make my re- introduction back into society," Michael stated.

"Why can't we stay and help?" Lily asked.

"This is something I have to do by myself," Michael said, hoping that Lily and Nick would just leave and stop asking questions.

Lily and Nick understood, and left to make their own arrangements for Monday. This week was going to be a real test of their detective skills.

Michael felt bad for having to make Lily and Nick leave, but he knew it was for their own safety he was actually concerned. While Michael was alone, he made arrangements for his encounter with this evil creature. Michael knew this was something he could not share with his friends, because creatures from unknown areas could read minds and Michael did not want Lily or Nick to get hurt. The creature would not be able to read Michael's mind since he was part Taemite. Michael went into his secret room and unpacked a box that had a weapon that he had hidden in case of an emergency. This was definitely going to be such an emergency.

The weapon was a small black object. It looked like a normal TV remote control, but this was not anything normal. Even though this weapon was small, it was extremely deadly to any creature that came into contact with it. He sat down to read from his book about Taemites. This book contained many secrets on being able to destroy creatures.

The time was soon approaching when Michael was going to come face to face with a monster that he himself actually was. Even though he no longer appeared to look like a creature, deep down, Michael knew he always would be a monster. Now all he could do was to wait for his friends to return in order to begin this plan of attack and save Strapron from being taken over by evil creatures that wanted to kill all Taemites.

Monday morning came, and normally Lily would not be so eager to return to school, but today was different. She had an important task to fulfill this morning.

Lily rushed downstairs and ate her breakfast quickly and was out the door. She didn't even allow her mom any time to ask her why she was so excited to go to school.

Lily raced over to Nick's house so they could go over some of the plans that would be enacted today.

"Hi Nick." Lily said.

"Are you ready to start this investigation?" Nick asked.

"Ready or not, it's got to be done," Lily said.

During their normal ride to school, Lily seemed a little quiet.

"Lily, are you alright?" Nick asked.

"I'm fine. I'm just a little scared," Lily admitted.

"What? You're scared. Wow, I never thought I would hear you admit that!" Nick exclaimed.

"Well, it's nothing that I'm proud of, and, besides, I don't want to learn anything bad about Mrs. Smith. She's always been so nice to me," Lily said.

"Don't worry, Lily, you've got me and Michael. We are here to help," Nick said kindly.

"I know. You're right, I'm just being silly. We'd better get going, I can't be late for my first class," Lily said.

Lily and Nick arrived at school and together walked in to begin this quest for answers.

Lily went straight to Mr. Wilkens class and sat down. Slowly the other students began arriving. The time had now come to put this plan into action.

Mr. Wilkens walked in and asked if anyone had come up with any more suggestions for the fundraiser. Lily abruptly threw her hand into the air.

"Lily, what's your idea?" Mr. Wilkens asked.

"I think we should have a school carnival. We had one a few years ago and it was very successful," Lily said, hoping Mr. Wilkens would take the bait. She waited.

Mr. Wilkens sat at his desk and didn't say anything. Lily was beginning to think maybe this wasn't going to work; when all of a sudden Mr. Wilkens stood up and said, "That's an excellent idea. What do the rest of you think?"

The students all cheered at this suggestion.

"Oh, yeah, Mr. Wilkens, my uncle is in town and wanted me to tell you that he is volunteering his time to help us," Lily said, still in detective mode.

"That's very nice of your uncle. I'm going to need a lot of help getting this carnival together. Make sure you tell your parents about this carnival and ask them if you can stay after school. This is going to take a lot of work. Do you all promise to stay after school and help make this carnival happen?"

All of the students agreed. The plan was now set into motion.

Later that day, Lily met Nick in the cafeteria to tell how him how successful the plan had worked.

"Nick, it worked. Mr. Wilkens agreed and he is ready to have Michael help us," Lily said excitedly.

"I hope we know what we're in for," Nick said, still a little worried that something bad was going to happen.

This week was going to be full of some major detective work.

Now had come the time for Michael to reenter society. Nick and Michael arrived at the school to put this plan into motion.

Once inside, Lily came up to them and brought them over to meet her new teacher. "Mr. Wilkens, this is my Uncle Michael," Lily said.

"Thank you so much for volunteering your time to help us," Mr. Wilkens responded.

"I think it's going to be fun." Michael said nervously.

"Michael, why don't you tell Mr. Wilkens about yourself," Lily added.

"Well, I'm from San Francisco. I used to work at a zoo, but I left to come here to write a book," Michael said, feeling pleased he was able to remember his lines.

Lily noticed as Michael said he was from San Francisco that Mr. Wilkens had a smile on his face.

"Michael, this is such a coincidence. I just moved here from San Francisco also. Maybe we met. You do look a little familiar to me," Mr. Wilkens asked.

Feeling like there cover was about to be revealed, Lily jumped into action. "Mr. Wilkens, where do you want us to start?" Lily asked.

"Why don't you all work on the dunking booth," Mr. Wilkens said.

As the three worked, the conversation quickly turned to Mr. Wilkens.

"I thought for sure he recognized me!" Michael said.

"Yeah, so did I," Lily replied.

While Nick, Michael, and Lily were busy working on the booth, Mr. Wilkens walked over.

"Lily why don't you come with me. I have something else I want you to do," Mr. Wilkens ordered.

Not wanting to blow their cover, Lily went with him. Lily had that feeling that always warned her when something bad was about to happen and boy was she ever getting it now.

"Nick, I want you to stay here. I'm going to follow them and make sure Lily's okay," Michael said, as he very slowly removed a pen-like object and pointed it at Nick.

This happened so fast that Nick was not even aware it even happened. Nick was getting really worried about Lily, and after a few minutes, he decided he needed to search for his best friend, but when Nick went to move, he was frozen. Lily was not the only one in need of rescue.

Mr. Wilkens took Lily into his classroom.

"What are we going to do in here?" Lily asked, as she took a deep breath.

"Lily, I know you remember me from Strapron," Jesper said.

"So it really is you? What are you doing in Scott City?" Lily asked.

"I'm here to finish what I started in Strapron. Lily, you're a smart girl and you know what has to happen," Jesper said.

"Why are you in Scott City pretending to be a teacher?" Lily asked.

"I guess it's alright to tell you everything now; you see I have some help that is going to meet us in Denver. Together we are going to use all of my students to help us take control of Strapron." Jesper confessed.

"Why would all of the students help you kill anything?" Lily continued in her questioning of this bad creature.

"We have a transformer that will turn humans into mechanical trolls. They will obey whatever we want them to do," Jesper said with a cocky smile on his face.

"How are you going to take over Strapron?" Lily asked.

"I am very close to Chief Leon, and with his power we will rule whatever we choose, including Earth!" Jesper said.

"Who is Leon?" Lily asked.

"Oh, I think you already know him," Jesper continued, pulling Lily into his web of tricks.

"I don't know him. Tell me now!" Lily ordered.

"Maybe later, but now I have some work that needs to be taken care of immediately," Jesper said angrily. Jesper opened his jacket and removed a silver canister.

"What's that?" Lily asked.

"Just wait," Jesper said, knowing that Michael was approaching.

Within seconds Michael was in the same room as this wicked creature.

"Michael, help me, he's going to use all of the students to take control over Strapron!" Lily yelled. Now fate was about to take a horrible twist in Lily's life.

"What took you so long?" Jesper said to Michael.

Lily's heart sank in disbelief. *It couldn't be, not Michael. He was her friend. Michael wouldn't do something as cruel as this.*

"I had to make sure Nick was not going to get in the way," Michael said.

"What did you do to Nick!" Lily screamed. "Michael, why would you do this? You are good! Why?" Lily asked with complete and utter doubt.

"Lily, it was all an act. You have been chosen. Just like I was chosen," Michael told his captured friend.

"What, why would I be chosen? I'm just a normal girl," Lily confessed.

"Lily, it's because of your dreams. You have a gift, and with that you have the possibility of endless power; that is, with the right training," Michael replied.

"We need to get this over before anyone gets in our way!" ordered Jesper. Jesper opened the silver canister and out came a cloud of green smoke. Within seconds, the smoke cleared the room and there stood Paglen.

"Paglen, what are you doing here?" Lily asked, now in even more disbelief that not only was Michael evil, but now her new friend Paglen was as well. All of a sudden Lily remembered something her grandpa had told her. If you ever find yourself in a dangerous situation, remain calm. Most captors can be tricked. "How can I use my dreams to become powerful?" Lily asked, hoping these creatures might fall into her trap.

"With the right training, you can rule whatever land you want. Not only Strapron, but anywhere," Jesper stated.

Paglen came close to Lily and gave her a look that made Lily understand that nothing was really what it seemed to be.

Meanwhile, Nick was working frantically on escaping from his own capture. Time stood still. There seemed no way that Nick was going to be able to free himself so he could help his friends. Somehow, Nick managed to gain some control in his left hand, but how could that be? Suddenly, Nick remembered that in his back pocket of his jeans he had brought the lazenfront necklace. Lazenfront was harmful to Taemites and was slowly releasing Nick from his frozen state. Slowly Nick pulled the necklace out, and within seconds the magic that had been used on him was gone. Finally free, Nick ran off in search of Lily.

Lily continued working on her plan of tricking these evil creatures that she was ready and willing to help in their plan of taking over Strapron and killing all Taemites. As Jesper walked up to Lily, she knew this might be the last time she could convince her captors of her loyalty towards them. "Michael, can you teach me your magic and I can teach you how to unleash your own power of dreams?" Lily asked.

"If I teach you, then you can never return to Scott City or to your family," Michael said.

"Michael, you are my family," Lily said, trying hard not to cry.

"Very well, release her!" ordered Michael.

"No, she can't be trusted!" yelled Jesper.

Michael grew very angry and took out the remote control item he had brought with him.

"What is that?" Lily asked.

Suddenly, Jesper let out a loud roar and quickly returned to his creature-like form. Once again, standing before Lily was the dragon that had captured her in Strapron.

Michael pointed this strange item at Jesper and with a matter of second Jesper was gone. Lying on the floor where Jesper once stood was a pile of blue powdered ash. "What did you do to him?" Lily asked.

"I put an end to his plan. I don't need him anymore. I have you right where I need you," Michael said as he walked closer to Paglen. "Paglen, I want you to hold Lily down for me. This is going to hurt," Michael ordered.

Paglen moved slowly to where poor Lily was being restrained.

Standing right outside of the door was Nick. He had heard all of this commotion and now knew what he had to do. Without thinking about how dangerous this was going to be, Nick went running into the room.

Michael turned around and saw Nick had escaped from his capture. "How did you get loose?" Michael asked.

"I remembered I had this!" Nick screamed, as he grabbed a hold of the necklace and ran toward Michael. Nick stabbed Michael in his chest with the very object that started this whole adventure from the summer. The lazenfront necklace finally put an end to the evil, including Michael.

Just as Nick was about to attack Paglen, Lily yelled. "No, Nick, not Paglen. He's here to help us!"

Paglen slowly approached Lily and Nick. "I'm so sorry I couldn't tell you about Michael. I knew who he was when he first found me in Strapron. I managed to befriend him. It took a while, but I finally gained his trust," Paglen confessed.

"So how is Mrs. Smith involved in this entire evil scheme?" Lily questioned.

Paglen raised his arms above his head, and right before their eyes Paglen turned into Mrs. Smith.

"You are Mrs. Smith?" Nick asked, unable to believe his own eyes.

"Yes, you see, I've been trying to put an end to Michael and Jesper for a long time now," Paglen revealed.

"Paglen, I don't know how we can ever thank you for everything you've done for us!" Lily exclaimed.

"There is one thing I would like you both to do for me," Paglen asked.

"Anything," Nick and Lily said together.

"Promise me you won't visit Strapron ever again," Paglen said.

Looking at each other, both Nick and Lily agreed.

Paglen returned to Strapron, while Lily and Nick returned home.

Although Nick believed in his promise that he had made to Paglen, Lily knew that the chances were good that she would one day return to Strapron, at least to visit her true friend, Paglen.

The adventures that Lily and Nick had endured during the summer were exciting, but not quite as thrilling as the beginning of the school year...